AT MY GENERAL'S COMMAND
MEN OF FORT DALE

ROMEO ALEXANDER

ROMEO ALEXANDER

Published by Books Unite People LLC, 2020.
Copyright © 2020 by Books Unite People
All rights reserved.

No part of this book may be reproduced in any form or by any electronic means, including information storage and retrieval systems, without written permission from the author, except for the use of brief quotations in a book review.

This book is a work of fiction. All resemblance to persons living or dead is purely coincidental.

Editing by Jo Bird

DAVID

Throbbing pulsed through his forehead as David stared at the screen. Grunting in annoyance, he pulled his attention away from the computer and began rooting through the drawers. They were far more cluttered than the top of the desk, and he cursed himself for not organizing them. Whenever he had a free moment, he was inevitably pulled into something.

Despite digging through the drawers, he found nothing to alleviate the pain. He would have to send his receptionist to find something, but he'd prefer not to. The moment he alerted Christian that something was wrong, the younger man would switch to nanny mode, and David wouldn't get any peace until he'd dealt with the problem.

To everyone else at Fort Dale, David was General Winter. As the man in charge of everything on the base, General David Winter did not expect much resistance from anyone. Yet his receptionist gave him shit like nobody's business and had a strange way of making David feel compelled to obey him.

It was irritating.

Flashing on his computer screen brought his head up, squinting at the display. His sister's face popped up with a shaking phone symbol. For a moment, he considered letting it go to voicemail. But Sara wouldn't stop calling if he didn't at least show some measure of attention. His older sister was laid back, but when she wanted to talk to him, nothing would deter her, not even him.

Sighing, he tapped the screen, answering the call with a faint *'boop'* from the speakers. He frowned as another window opened, displaying his sister's face and the kitchen behind her. David had only a moment to see something cooking on the stove in the background before she adjusted the camera so her face filled the whole screen.

She arched a thin brow. "Wow, you answered on the first call? I'm shocked."

David curled his lip. "What choice did I have? It was either answer now or have you pester me until I did."

"I see you're learning," Sara chuckled.

"I've been bullied, harassed, and beaten down. I've learned my lesson."

"Harassed. That's putting it a little dramatically, don't you think?"

"I notice you didn't object to bullied or beaten down, however."

"Well, no, I can't argue with the truth."

David snorted. "What can I do for you, Sara?"

Her brow stitched together. "Really? You're going to ask that? It's been over a month since we last spoke, David."

Squinting faintly, he ran the numbers through his head and winced as he realized his sister had been generous. It had been closer to two months, and even then, Sara had reached out to him.

"Ah, hell, I'm sorry. Things have been a little chaotic

lately, and it seems a few things slipped the net," David explained.

"Your sister included. Also, you look like shit."

David scowled. "Thank you so much."

Her comment, however, drew his attention to the little square in the upper corner of the call window. The head of once thick onyx-black hair was almost fifty-fifty salt and pepper. There were a few lines around the dark circles beneath his pale green eyes and a few more around his lips than there had been ten years ago. Still, he didn't think he looked that bad for a man on his way to forty-six.

"And I look just fine," David finally said.

Sara laughed. "You do, but I made you look."

"What are you, five?"

"No, just not a stick in the mud."

Despite being the oldest, his sister was young at heart. Sara was the first to laugh and quick with a joke to make someone else smile. Their mother had always insisted she take things more seriously and then begrudgingly said Sara would learn one day...maybe. By the time their mother passed, she had long since given up hope that Sara would ever 'grow up.'

David thought that was a little unfair. Despite the pitfalls she had fallen into, she'd done well for herself. David wasn't sure what she'd got up to at college, but she'd come out of it with a major in education and taught at a high school in Houston. While her love life had been tumultuous, she'd met, married, and settled down with Ryan, and their three kids were doing great.

"You do look a little tired," Sara said, interrupting his mental wandering.

"I always look tired to you."

"Yeah, and?"

There wasn't much he could say about that; he usually *was* tired. If their mother had wished Sara was more serious, David was the epitome of everything their mother wanted in a child. Their father had referred to him as an old soul, claiming David had always been quiet and studious even before he could talk. He looked at things with a measured approach, whether schoolwork or basic training and MOS training in the military.

"These days, tiredness is a state of being, not an odd occurrence. You should know that by now," David told her.

Sara shook her head. "You're the oldest forty-five-year-old I know, David. You need a vacation."

He was overdue for time off, but every time he thought about taking a week or two, something came up. His plate was currently pretty full, and he couldn't imagine what it would look like if he had to put it all off for a while.

"And leave this place to fall apart? I think not."

Sara raised her brow again. "Don't you have people who can handle things for a few weeks while you blow off steam?"

"In theory."

"But not in practice?"

David cringed, not wanting to divulge too much. The problem was that the person next in line, Philip Rogan, was not the sort of man David wanted running Fort Dale day-to-day. Rogan was a decent enough administrator, but he wouldn't be David's first choice to run the whole base.

"Still having problems with Phil?" Sara asked knowingly.

"I wouldn't describe it as a problem."

"If you're unwilling to let him do his job because you don't trust him, I'd call that a problem."

It was both a fair and unfair assessment. Rogan could cope well enough, but David didn't trust him to do things right. Rogan had joined the military in peacetime, not when the nation was at war, and knew nothing about what it was like to be a soldier, in David's opinion. Trained and growing up in peacetime had created a politician out of the man in charge of Operations, and David was loathed to put his trust in someone who looked at the men and women at Fort Dale as little more than numbers to be crunched.

"I thought you were going to take care of that at some point," Sara continued.

David snorted, looking at his screen where his to-do list sat open. The damn thing was so long it required him to scroll to reach the bottom. There was too much at Fort Dale that needed addressing, and he found himself adding things more than subtracting them.

"It's on the list," David said with a gesture.

"The ever-growing list that's going to send you right to an early grave. That one?"

"I'll have you know I'm in good shape. My last check-up went without a single new comment to worry about."

"Meaning your blood pressure is still sky-high."

David shifted uncomfortably. "It's a tad high."

"Which you refuse to take medication for or lower your workload."

"Is this a conversation or an inquisition?" David demanded.

Sara frowned at the screen. "You know damn well I'm worried about you."

"There's no need to worry. I'm not in any danger of a heart attack or stroke. I'm eating well, and I always make time each day to exercise."

"You're also sleeping like absolute shit and have a workload that would give a dedicated workaholic gray hair at the thought of it."

"Well, that's not fair, I sleep just fine. I'm just not getting much sometimes."

"David."

"What? There's a difference."

Sara shook her head. "I love how you only develop a sense of humor when you want to be a smartass."

"This from the woman who won't give anything a rest until she hears she's right. I feel more pity for Ryan every time we have one of these...fun conversations of ours."

Sara smirked. "I promise he has ways of shutting me up."

"Oh, God."

And if the devilish look on his sister's face was any warning, he knew exactly where this conversation was heading.

David held his finger out in warning. "Do not."

Sara, predictably, ignored him. "So, my dear, sweet little brother, whatever happened to that love life you were supposedly getting ready to have?"

David groaned, giving up all pretense of dignity and flopping his head back to cover his face. He'd made the mistake last time they'd spoken of telling his sister he had a date. His complete silence afterward must have caught her interest, and he should have known it would eventually come up.

"Things did not work out," David muttered.

"And what was wrong with this one?" Sara asked.

"Nothing, it just...didn't work out. There doesn't have to be a reason every time. Some things just don't work."

"Right, because the woman before that one was too much of a hermit."

"As a man who's expected to go to cocktail parties, galas, charity functions, and the like, having someone social by my side isn't an unfair expectation," David told her.

"And the guy before that wasn't serious enough."

"Anyone who thinks it's perfectly acceptable to drink themselves stupid on a work night, more than once a week, is not someone I need in my life, Sara."

"Okay, fair point. You made it sound like it was only once."

"He and I talked for a couple of weeks, and he informed me it had happened four times."

"Wasn't he my age?"

"Yes."

Sara wrinkled her nose. "Alright, you win that one."

"Nice to know I can win something with you," he said dryly.

"But that doesn't change the fact that it *is* about time you stopped being so damn difficult and tried a little romance in your life."

It wasn't a new argument. Along with his sister's zest for life and insistence on tackling every problem head-on, her passion for romance and love had not been diminished. That wasn't to say David didn't have aspirations for a companion.

"You and I both know I've made several attempts to date in the past two and a half decades, Sara," David reminded her.

"For someone with a larger dating pool than most, you have a harder time finding someone than anyone I know."

David frowned. "That's not fair. And my pool is not bigger."

"Right, being interested in men and women doesn't open things up more."

"A heterosexual woman does not exactly suffer from a dearth of choice," David said dryly.

That and the pool got narrower when people he considered dating found out he was bisexual. Twenty years ago, he would have understood people's reluctance to date a bisexual man considering the mentality toward men being attracted to men and would have begrudgingly accepted it ten years ago. Yet there was still an ugly stigma around being a bisexual man, even as acceptance of gay men was becoming the norm.

"And need I remind you of the handful of men and

women who immediately 'lost' my number or whatever, when they found out I was into men and women?" David asked.

Sara wrinkled her nose. "At least you were spared having to find out they were an asshole further down the line, right?"

"Not the point."

"The point is you can't keep using excuses to avoid it."

"You are aware I have a full schedule, right? If I can't take time off for a vacation, what makes you think I have time for a relationship?"

"You can make time. You just don't want to."

David sighed. "What was the point of this call again?"

"To check on you and to go full worrying sister on you."

"Thank you. Between you and my receptionist, I'm quite well covered."

Sara's eyes lit up. "Oh, Christian? He's cute."

David's eyes darted to his message icon, which had blipped with an unread notification. He could see where his sister's delight was leading, and he was not ashamed to take a moment to leave the conversation before she tried to find a new avenue to harass him.

"Yes, Christian. Speaking of, he's just messaged me, and I'm going to assume it has something to do with my job. So, if you'll excuse me, I really should get going," David said.

Sara smirked. "Have you really got a message from him, or are you just trying to get off the phone with me?"

David snorted. "The amazing thing about my job, dear sister, is that I am more than capable of multitasking. So I can do my job and use it as an excuse to escape this conversation."

Sara laughed, waving a hand at him. "Fine, you can run, but you can't hide."

"Love you," David said, ending the call.

Shaking his head, he opened Christian's message to see if he was right about it being important. Reading the contents, he realized his receptionist had put off his next appointment because the system had told him David was on a private call. Shaking his head, David replied, telling him to send his next appointment in and to alert him next time rather than putting it off.

He opened the files for the scheduled meeting. Out of the dozens of problems that cropped up every day, David was desperate to bring the current team of specialized soldiers back to full strength. Team Maelstrom desperately needed help and a team member to fill their ranks. As much as David despised having to shove a new member onto the team, only a few months after the men had lost one of their own in battle, his hands were tied.

When his door opened, David took a moment to arrange everything on his screen for ease of use. He already had a good idea of what he wanted to say to the Sergeant, but it never hurt to have notes on hand.

"Sergeant Rider," David said by way of greeting.

The soldier snapped a salute. "General Winter."

David looked up, immediately noticing how exhausted Sergeant Aidan Rider looked. The man had been thrown from the desert and then to the other side of the country in the same week. It was amazing that he could even stand up. His expression was impossible to read, but David watched as the man's eyes swept the room quickly before resting on David's face again, watching him, observing.

David waved a hand toward the chairs. "At ease. Make yourself comfortable."

Maybe when this was over, he could get Christian to order some food along with finding some damn pain relievers. The man knew the best places to find good food, and David had yet to be disappointed.

CHRISTIAN

Humming to himself, Christian stepped from the elevator onto the second floor. The room, which served as his workplace and appointment waiting room, lit up as the sensors caught his movement. It wasn't an ornate room, angled more toward comfort than anything else.

The plush couches against one wall and the soft chairs against the other were suitable for those who had to cool their heels. He didn't imagine the natural wood-colored floors or the soft blue walls, did much to calm the nerves of those left to wait. It was a fact of life at Fort Dale, however, that those without an appointment had to wait, and sometimes, even those who did still had to cool their heels.

The only furniture that could be called fancy was the huge desk at the back. Christian wasn't sure if General Winter had ordered a desk made of genuine marble or if it had a convincing veneer over a wooden one, but the effect was immediate. In the first few weeks, as General Winter's personal assistant, the monstrous desk seemed to be some foreboding obelisk placed at the entrance to a cursed cave. It took up most of the back wall. Nearly everyone who came to the office found the desk came up to about chest height. Christian had to use a tall chair to look over it, which was saying something since he wasn't exactly short.

He rounded the desk and set his travel mug of coffee down. Being just past six am, the office was quiet. General Winter wouldn't be in for another hour, which gave him plenty of time to do his prep work. The general had made several changes over the past few years to the fort's computer system. While the systems worked wonders to simplify almost everyone's job, Christian still preferred the personal touch.

"Good morning, ladies," Christian said to the array of simple cloth dolls on his desk.

Unsurprisingly, the dolls said nothing, staring back at him with their huge, black-felt eyes as he hit the power button on his computer. They were crude things, and a few people who spotted them said they found them a little creepy. Christian wasn't that fond of the dolls either, but the hastily made caricatures of his two sisters would never bring him anything but warmth.

As if on cue, his phone buzzed quietly in his pocket. While Christian waited for the computer to boot up, he pulled the device out and checked it. Only one person he could think of would be awake at such an early hour and messaging him.

P sure Dan is avoiding me rn.

Christian shook his head at Lily's message. The woman never knew when to leave well enough alone, especially when a guy she was dating was involved. Her passion and romantic ideals had already been locked into her personality when Christian had met her. They'd both been thirteen. The twelve years that followed had done nothing to blunt the woman's determination to find herself a man and hold him down.

Shaking his head, Christian typed back.

Have you tried letting him have a bit of room? Can't smother the guy.

It took only a minute before her response was fired back.

It's been two days that's not smothering.

Christian shook his head, typing back a message reminding her that the man worked two jobs, one full-time and one part-time. He turned his attention back to his computer and logged in. The system took a moment to check its records before a confirmation screen popped up. It was always his least favorite part of the process, as the confirmation screen always involved a picture of himself and his ID number.

The picture had been taken after a particularly harrowing couple of days where Christian had been run ragged as he'd tried to settle in at Fort Dale. The circles under his eyes had been so dark they'd nearly obscured the bright blue color. Even his blond hair, usually so bright it looked almost gold, had seemed to lose its luster and had grown just a shade too far past regulation. His narrow jaw and high cheekbones were lost in the general pale look of his skin from exhaustion and an overly bright camera flash.

Rather than look at the screen with the god-awful picture, he turned his gaze back to his phone.

Just cuz he's busy doesn't mean he can't message me once.

Sighing, Christian opened the message and tapped back.

It does if the poor guy is exhausted. Give him a break. And don't blow his phone up either.

With the computer logged in, he set his phone aside and began reviewing what new messages awaited him. There were the standard emails sent directly to him, and then the messages which were sent down the chain from Command. There was nothing of any real note, so he moved on to the inbox reserved for General Winter. His access to General

Winter's messages was limited to the same general and personal emails as his inbox. General Winter had granted access to Christian months ago to try and create some order out of the chaos that liked to flood his inbox.

Christian scrolled past an email from General Winter's sister, Sara, and moved to a message from the general's bank. He wouldn't read anything deeply personal, but since he was generally the first to realize when General Winter was missing a due date on a bill or an update from a business he might need to know, Christian typically read anything that looked important.

As he expected, his phone began to buzz *constantly* once the clock hit half-past six. Christian tapped the Bluetooth in his ear to answer the call without looking at the device.

"Good morning, Lily," he said.

"I can't believe you're taking his side," she said in greeting.

Christian laughed, deleting the bank email. "You've been blowing up his phone, haven't you?"

"Oh, come on, you and I both know he's not taking the time to talk to me."

Christian shrugged, reaching to open the new message in his inbox. "He might be, he might not be. But if he is, pestering him isn't going to do you any good. He's going to keep ignoring you. If he's just busy and tired, then all you're doing is driving him away."

"I still say it's not hard to send one text in forty-eight hours to let me know he's alive."

He'd known Lily for a dozen years, and he knew damn well there was no point in trying to change her mind when she was determined and set on a course. He also knew it was better to distract her before she picked up steam. Once Lily got going, there was no bringing her back until she ran out of energy, which could take the better part of an hour if she was really riled.

"How's Mary?" Christian asked.

"Don't think you can distract me."

"I'm asking about our sister because the last I heard from her, she wasn't feeling too good."

Lily sighed. "She had to stay home yesterday, but don't worry. When I saw her last night before I headed out for my shift, she was up and didn't look so bad."

Christian frowned. "Not looking bad isn't quite the same as being okay."

"She was making dinner and reading, so I'd take that as a good sign."

Christian snorted. "And since you don't know how she was feeling, I'm guessing she wasn't talking about it."

"Nope, and you know what that means."

"It means she was feeling less like death."

"Exactly."

It had been a little while since Mary's last episode, and Christian was relieved to hear it was brief. Christian had met Mary when he'd been fourteen, and it had been a few months before he'd seen her go through the agony that she had, at the time, called 'headaches.' At first, the doctors thought she was having migraines, odd for a girl of fifteen but not unheard of. It wasn't until a few years ago that someone had finally diagnosed her with cluster headaches.

There were treatments, but they didn't make the headaches stay away for good. All they did was decrease their frequency and make them not last as long. It still didn't stop her from feeling like rusty nails were tearing apart her entire head. She swore up and down it was better to spend a day or two like that every few months rather than days in agony every few weeks. Christian had to agree, but it still hurt to see her in so much pain that she couldn't function.

"I'll call her later when I'm off my shift. Maybe she'll be less stubborn if I talk to her."

"Yeah, yeah, I know. I'm pushy, and people don't want to talk to me like they do you."

Christian chuckled. "I think it's because you guys are just...both stubborn. You won't stop, and she won't give in."

"I don't think that's totally true," Lily said slowly.

"Right, because I haven't watched the two of you go at it over the years or anything, you're right."

"Sarcasm isn't cute, Christian."

Christian grinned, motioning at himself even though he was alone. "Good thing I'm adorable enough to make it cute, huh?"

"I see someone's coffee has started kicking in."

"As if I need it."

"Yeah, a regular bundle of sunshine and energy you are."

"Says the woman who wakes up ready to sing half the time."

"I just...get songs stuck in my head, is all."

Christian's laugh almost muffled the sound of the elevator. He checked the computer screen and sighed. General Winter was early, but Christian was used to that.

"Ah, the general is here," Christian warned his sister.

"Ooh, General Daddy?" Lily cooed.

"Oh, God, shut up."

He carefully arranged his face so it didn't look like he was on the phone as the doors slid open to reveal the general. In all the months he'd been working directly under the man, Christian had never seen the general come into the office looking anything but perfectly put together. His uniform was always carefully pressed and neat, his hair had never been longer than it should be, and Christian was pretty sure he'd never seen him look groggy.

"Good morning, General," Christian said, keeping his voice warm but not too perky.

General Winter looked at him, the corner of his mouth turning up. "Good morning, Christian. Everything alright?"

Christian nodded, bringing up the day's schedule on his screen. "Everything's going smoothly so far. You'll be happy to know you don't have that busy a day."

General Winter snorted as he reached the desk. "Meaning, I'll be able to eat lunch without interruption."

"That about sums it up."

"Well, send the schedule to my screen, and I'll take a look."

Christian tapped a button. "Done."

"Not that it'll matter. You'll keep the ship afloat whether I see the schedule or not."

Christian tried not to look pleased at the compliment. For all the assholes with superiority complexes and a love of abusing power Christian had dealt with in the service, he was pleased to find there were still men like General Winter in charge. The general was a good man, a bit too serious, but a man who believed in doing right by the men and women serving under him and was not shy with a compliment or a criticism when either was called for.

"I'd rather be out here keeping things neat and trim than dealing with everyone like you do, General," Christian said.

"Good, because I'm sure it would look like a disaster if I had your job."

Christian restrained the urge to contradict him. General Winter was dedicated to his job, and Christian suspected that would translate to whatever the older man was doing. Christian considered it an honor to help the general get through his day as smoothly as possible. If that meant doing everything from structuring his schedule to something as mundane as ordering food and cleaning out his inbox, he was happy to do it.

Lily's voice came through the Bluetooth again. "Oh, General Winter, please tell me how good a boy I am."

Christian held his smile as he unlocked the door to Winter's office with a press of a button. "I'll be sure to let you know if anything changes."

General Winter nodded, his eyes searching Christian's face. "I'm sure you will, thank you."

Despite his resistance to Lily's words and desperation not to be too obvious, Christian still found his eyes drifting after the man as he entered his office. For all the good things Christian could say about the man's personality, there was plenty more to be said about him physically. The general was not a man to rest on his laurels and, despite being in his upper forties, was in as good shape, if not better, than many of Christian's peers.

"You're looking at his ass, aren't you?" Lily asked.

Christian almost growled a response until General Winter popped his head back out. "And good morning to your sister as well."

Christian waited until the door was shut before speaking. "You are absolutely impossible."

Lily laughed. "God, he said good morning to me. My day is complete."

"Lily, please," Christian moaned.

He hadn't known it at the time, but having his foster sisters come to the base had been a terrible mistake. It had been four months since their visit, but all it had taken was one glimpse of General Winter for Lily to remember and never let go. It hadn't helped that she was the only one to see the lingering look Christian gave the older man, greeting Christian as he'd passed.

"Damn, I wish I got to see that every day. My boss is greasy from head to toe, and I don't think he knows what a toothbrush is."

Christian drew up the day's schedule he'd created the

night before. "And on that oh-so-delicious note, I'm afraid I have to bid you good night, dear sister."

"It's seven am."

"Good night to you and the rest of the third shifters of the world."

"AKA, shut the hell up, Lily, and let me get to work?"

"Something like that."

"That's fine. I've made it home anyway. I'll tell Mary to expect a call from you later as I pass her in the living room."

"Like two ships in the night," Christian said.

"Well, at least we have you as a lighthouse."

Christian smiled. "Love you too."

He hung up, turning his attention back to the rest of his morning routine. Returning messages and fiddling with the schedules for the rest of the week kept him occupied despite the dull ache of loneliness and homesickness that had settled deep in his chest.

DAVID

It was one of the few days David didn't need to rush back to the office immediately after a meeting. He decided to take a walk. His stomach was contentedly full from lunch an hour before, and the day was beautiful. He walked through parts of the base each week to see how everything was going without interfering.

He'd come to Fort Dale almost a decade before, a freshly promoted general ready to take on the world. It amused him to think that even a man in his late thirties could still have the same naive confidence and optimistic enthusiasm of a man ten years his junior. Every few years, when he looked back on his life, he wondered how his past self could have been so blind.

Yet as he walked under the warm sun, feeling the breeze from the nearby ocean, he didn't regret his choices. David had been given a chance to exist outside the usual politics and crap of dealing with others and given command of his own base. It had been a risky move by the higher-ups, entrusting an entire base to the command of a young general who had yet to prove themselves. David had relished getting his hands dirty, so to speak, and to prove to himself and others that he was more than fit for the job.

Sure, there were still plenty of things on his list to fix. Operations was still a bit of a mess, and more often than not, David had to take control and ensure training was running smoothly and that any soldiers coming from outside the base were properly cared for. He still had to contend with the occasional complaint from the nearby town when they had to deal with a soldier getting drunk and aggressive on a night off. Yet, all in all, he considered he had fulfilled his wish to be a success.

His phone trilled softly, pulling him out of his thoughts. It was the tone reserved for Christian. He wasn't sure how the man had set it up, but when it came to the ins and outs of the system, David had made sure was installed at Fort Dale, Christian knew most of it.

Philip is supposed to be showing up in an hour.

David grimaced, knowing he had to cut his tour short to be prepared for that meeting. Any sit-down with Philip was usually twice as long as needed and half as efficient as it should be. Resigned to his fate, he tapped a message back to Christian.

Understood. And you are aware he has a title, correct?

Christian's response came back so quickly David would have thought the younger man was using an actual keyboard.

Yeah. Why, what are you going to do, report me?

That brought a soft laugh from David, who pocketed his phone rather than responding and encouraging Christian. It was probably not a good idea, at least professionally speaking, to let his receptionist show him what could be called disrespect, especially since it had begun with Christian referring to a superior by his first name without his proper rank and title.

Yet, it was a small pleasure for David to have someone

like Christian around. Everyone else he dealt with, save his sister, treated him as General Winter, a man to be respected and spoken to carefully. There was the occasional unruly soldier who ignored that, but General Winter knew full well how to throw his weight around if necessary. With Christian, David knew there was no disrespect from the younger man when he spoke flippantly or even when he harassed David. If anything, there was a playful casualness David welcomed in his otherwise stiff and formulaic life.

But he also wasn't so foolish as to encourage the man more than necessary.

When he returned to the office, Christian was seated behind his desk, as usual, popping something from a small plastic bag into his mouth. When David grew closer, he realized the snacks were, in fact, carrots, and he couldn't help but smile smugly.

"I see you decided to take my advice," David said.

Christian sighed. "Yes, General Winter, after your repeated...reminders, I decided I could incorporate a few healthy snacks into my meals."

"Sounds like a polite way of saying I nagged you," David pointed out.

"I would never be so bold as to accuse my superior of being a nag," Christian said, batting his eyelashes.

The gesture was affected and not meant to be taken seriously. Yet David couldn't help noticing the slight pull in his gut. Along with finding the man's personality absolutely endearing, there was something about the entire package. David would have been a liar if he tried to tell himself he wasn't occasionally drawn to men a decade or two younger than he was.

"No, you wouldn't, but you'd be willing to insinuate it strongly when there's no one around to hear you," David said.

Christian winked, popping another carrot into his mouth with a crunch. "I might be guilty of that sort of shady behavior occasionally."

David chuckled. "So, what time is my Operations leader supposed to be showing up?"

"You mean your Operations leader *at the moment*, right?" Christian asked with a raised brow.

David frowned. "Have you been reading my outbound messages again?"

Christian sighed. "I'm sorry, yes. I thought General Pollack wanted another one of your recipes when I saw the message. Didn't realize it was work-related. I told you to mark any emails I'm not supposed to see, but you never do."

That was true. "You didn't need to keep reading it once you saw what it contained."

Christian wrinkled his nose. "Once I realized, I stopped reading. But it was too late. Cat was out of the bag. You're trying to get Philip transferred."

David cleared his throat. "That you're privy to the information is fine, I suppose. But I'd prefer that you didn't talk about it openly, thank you."

Christian winked. "You got it. Lord knows keeping my mouth shut is a skill I've had to master over the years."

David cocked his head, wondering why Christian felt the need to say, 'years,' rather than just 'year.' Christian had been placed directly under David about a year ago, and working the front desk required discretion. Not just because Christian was exposed to David's life but because of the problematic soldiers he dealt with, and when Command showed up.

However, his question was tossed aside as Christian put down the carrots and linked his arms behind his head. He leaned back in his seat, letting out a low groan as he stretched the muscles in his back. It had the unintended side effect of making the front of his uniform ride up, showing a flash of bare skin and the pale blond hair of his stomach. Once again, David felt that pull in his gut, but much harder than before.

"The water Philip is so fond of is already in your office fridge, and he was nice enough to mention that he just wanted to 'catch up' on things. So, I took the notes you gave me from the last meeting, mixed them with what's changed since then, and created a little cheat sheet. Maybe it'll be good enough to get you through the meeting faster than usual," Christian said as he dropped his feet on the ground and stared at his computer again.

David nodded, thankful, and shoved aside the image of Christian's bare skin and the question of what the rest of him looked like. In a strange quirk, he liked his men younger than him but his women older. He knew damn well that if Christian was not firmly off-limits, David would be sorely tempted to try and find out what the rest of Christian's pale skin looked like. But he was Christian's superior, and there were strict rules about fraternization, particularly regarding generals.

"I'll give it a look over and try not to consider dipping into the case full of liquor I have in there," David said, rounding the desk once he thought it was safe to expose the front of his uniform.

Christian chuckled. "I'll even be a good boy and warn you what kind of mood he's in. I'm hoping for all business. If he's jolly, he likes to stand around and chat before he comes in to see you."

"Oh, the horror," David said dryly as he pushed into his office.

* * *

Predictably, Philip was late. A full twenty minutes after the arranged time, David received a notification from Christian that Philip had arrived. It took another ten minutes before the next message told him Philip was on his way in. David took that to mean Philip was particularly happy and had lingered to chat with Christian. The addition at the end of Christian's message raised David's brow.

Seems a little too happy if you ask me.

David wasn't sure what that meant, but he didn't have time to contemplate it. The door to his office swung open, and Philip strolled in, or more accurately, strutted in. Philip Rogan enjoyed living big and did everything with as much expression and confidence as he could muster. Where someone else would walk, he would strut. Where they would talk, he would proclaim. Most of the time, David ignored it and let the man say whatever he had to, praying he would get through the meeting before the day was supposed to end.

"Phil, good to see you," David said, standing up to take the man's hand.

Philip grinned wide, shaking David's hand briskly. "David, a pleasure as always. I hope you've been well?"

"As well as can be expected," David said, gesturing to the seats.

Philip dropped into one. David didn't require formality from those he worked closely with, and next to Philip's desire to seem at ease with everything, there was a casualness between them that went quite far.

Much of that informal relationship came from David being responsible for Philip's continued contract with the military. A few years before, there had been a quiet but substantial incident that could have cost Philip everything. David, out of pity for a man whose entire life depended on staying in the military, had quietly interceded. The situation had been swept under the rug, and Philip not only went unharmed but had even been, against David's private concerns, placed as the head of operations at Fort Dale.

A decision David hoped would soon be changed.

"Well enough, I suppose. Seems like there's always something needing my attention. I'm lucky to get my breath," David admitted as he sat down.

Philip let out a loud laugh. "Yes, I'm more than aware of what that feels like."

David chuckled, trying his best not to ask what exactly it was that kept Philip so damned busy. It certainly wasn't his job since David did half of it. Though he supposed it was hard work, staying on decent terms with the other generals and the rest of Command. Those connections had made it difficult for David to finally get someone to listen to him about replacing Philip, and hopefully with someone who might do the job better than David, whose attention was constantly divided.

It just required one more piece of the puzzle, one he would have to follow up with Christian after his meeting with Philip.

"It's been a bit since Sergeant Rider settled in. How's he getting on with the team?" David asked, knowing the answer since he'd seen the reports.

Philip wrinkled his nose. "Not well. I can't say I agree with your choice of an intel officer for Team Maelstrom, especially considering they've done nothing but argue since they met."

Well, two of them were arguing. It seemed the team leader and the new intelligence officer were not seeing eye to eye. Then again, David hadn't expected the transition to be smooth and wasn't bothered by the reports. The deep crease in Philip's brow told him he was bothered.

"Can't expect everything to go smoothly, especially with all that's happened with Maelstrom. Best to let them work things out on their own for a while. Just make sure the team leader knows to keep everyone busy, including himself," David said.

"If you say so, David. I don't think this will end well," Philip said, continuing to frown.

Which boiled down to regret on Philip's part for not having chosen in the first place and letting David do it instead. The difference between them, at least with the decision regarding the newest member of Team Maelstrom, was that Philip would have looked at the bottom line and picked what looked the best. David's approach had been to comb through the files of possible candidates, trying to get a good idea of each of the soldiers he was looking at and choose the one that *felt* right. His instincts, especially regarding command, had been right more often than not.

"Well, if that's the case, then I owe you an apology, and I have no problem taking the fall if this blows up in our faces," David soothed.

Philip laughed again. "But if it goes well instead?"

David snorted. "We both know Command isn't going to care one bit if it goes well. They only pay attention when things go to hell."

Philip slapped his knee. "Isn't that the damn truth? We've been up to our necks here, and they don't care as long as everything works out for them. At least you have Christian going for you, right?"

"He has been a great help, yes," David admitted.

"Ah, what I wouldn't give to have someone cute and nubile working my front desk. It would certainly liven my day up a bit," Philip said with a wink.

David shook his head. "That's hardly what I spend my day thinking about."

Most of the time.

"Still, doesn't hurt, eh?"

David decided it was time to change the subject before Philip tried to prod him. The last thing he needed was to have Philip bring Christian into a crude discussion. The thought grated on David's nerves, and he would have preferred Philip thought about Christian as little as possible.

"Well, it will please you to know you won't be floundering much longer," David said, opening a file on his computer.

Philip cocked his head. "Oh?"

"Well, this isn't the first time you've spoken of needing help. So I found you someone who can."

Philip blinked. "How...so?"

"You've said time and time again you could use some help, and what better than someone who knows their stuff? I found a man, Oscar Reyes, who could definitely benefit you but also could use the experience," David said, turning the computer screen to face Philip.

Philip's eyes turned cautious, though his smile remained. "You're...replacing the assistant I already have?"

"Your receptionist will be fine. Reyes will work directly under you and aid you with decision-making. He has a lot of field experience and has commanded more than his fair share of soldiers. His injuries prevent him from doing anything active, so I figured, take his field experience, combine it with your administrative talent, and we have a match made in heaven," David explained.

"I wasn't looking for a replacement," Philip said carefully.

David snorted. "Replacement? This man will help you."

And hopefully, replace him. David hated this aspect of his job, preferring to run the base instead of being neck-deep in politics. Yet it was an inevitable aspect of his life, and he couldn't avoid it forever. He had a feeling Reyes would be ten times better than Philip at the job and a hundred times more dedicated. All the man needed was to learn the ropes.

"Well, I'll certainly give it some thought," Philip said, the happiness surrounding him disappearing.

"He'll be arriving soon, so you'll have time to figure out how to integrate him. I'm sure we can find him something to do around here in the meantime," David said.

Not that Philip would have a whole lot of choice in the matter. If David wanted Philip to have someone working as what would essentially be a protégé, then that would happen. Philip didn't have to like it, and he could drag his heels and draw out Oscar's placement, but it would happen. Hopefully, once it did, with enough time, David might be able to present Reyes as a better choice and see if there wasn't something somewhere else that would suit Philip better.

Philip's attitude shifted almost immediately back to his previous mood, speaking loudly as he moved on to another subject. David nodded, adding only enough to keep Philip happy as the man began to regale him with a tale about a few unruly new soldiers and ideas for improving the clinic's efficiency. However, David did not need to engage much in the conversation, as Philip was perfectly happy to hear himself talk, allowing David to zone out peacefully.

That was until a message popped up on his screen, bearing Christian's name.

Good Lord, he's so loud. You're going to need a hearing aid if he keeps this up.

David kept his rapt expression, nodding to Philip as he replied.

Are you calling me old?

It took a moment, and David almost smirked at how long Christian took to answer.

There's no answer to that question that wouldn't get me in hot water, so I admit defeat.

David's lips twitched, and he closed the message thread, feeling better than he had moments before.

CHRISTIAN

Another day, another lunch at his desk. Christian wasn't going to complain, though, as it'd been a relatively quiet day for both he and General Winter. Most days, the two had to work through their lunch, taking bites when they could. Christian had no doubt it was worse for General Winter, as work for him generally involved meeting people. You couldn't exactly stuff your face while you were having a serious conversation with someone.

Then again, Christian couldn't say he did any better. Even with his workload lower than usual, he was still tapping away at his computer while he munched on his taco salad. Despite nothing on his to-do list that demanded immediate attention, he liked to keep on top of anything that might come up. Someone was always looking to make an appointment to see the general or follow up on a message he sent. The tasks built up quickly, and Christian liked to keep them arranged and prepared to be set into an appropriate schedule as quickly as possible.

And that didn't include the sudden changes, cancellations, and impromptu visits. Each had to be juggled to make it work for everyone. Christian had learned he would never make everyone happy, but he could try to minimize the number of pissed-off people.

He was interrupted when he heard the office door open, and General Winter poked his head out. Christian glanced over, watching the general look around the waiting room before disappearing into his office. Staring at the door, he considered messaging the man to find out if he needed something but was spared when General Winter reappeared, this time with his lunch in tow.

Christian stared at the plastic bowl. "Something wrong with it?"

General Winter shook his head, setting it on Christian's desk. "Not at all. You always get good food."

"Well, except for that one time when the Chinese hit us both wrong," Christian reminded him.

"Yes, and they still haven't stopped sending apology letters with coupons," General Winter said dryly.

"I know. I've used some of them for my lunch," Christian said as he popped another forkful into his mouth.

"I can't believe you've gone back to them," General Winter said.

Christian shrugged. "Everyone makes mistakes. Plus, their crab Rangoon is too good to pass up. It's the best I've ever tasted."

General Winter raised a brow. "I don't know if I've said it before, but why am I not surprised that someone as little as you is a food person?"

Christian looked down at his midsection with a frown. "Little? I'm not little."

Maybe he looked little to the general, who stood over six feet and had at least thirty, if not forty pounds on him, but Christian thought he did pretty well for himself. He'd settled at a perfectly reasonable five-foot-nine and, with a bit of work, managed to get close to almost one hundred seventy pounds.

Christian snorted. "I bet you also refer to me as a kid when I'm not around."

General Winter hesitated. "I can't say I've ever referred to you as a kid."

Hearing that made Christian smile warmly. General Winter had never treated him as anything but a capable adult, which is more than could be said for some people Christian had met in the general's age group. Not being seen as a kid made it far more comfortable for Christian to enjoy ogling the older man when he had the chance. He might know damn well that he had to keep his hands to himself, but that didn't mean he couldn't enjoy the view. And if the general didn't make it strange by seeing him as a kid or some sort of son figure, then all the better for Christian's fantasies.

"Well, that's good, but I still reserve the right to color on my off time," Christian told him.

"You color?"

Christian nodded. "I get a good coloring session in now and again. It was something cheap for my foster parents to buy me. Of course, now, as an adult, I can buy good colored pencils."

"Colored pencils, huh?"

"Colored pencils are the superior coloring tool, and no one can change my mind. Trust me, my sisters have tried."

"Clearly, they don't have any taste."

"That's what I keep telling them!"

General Winter chuckled, shaking his head. "And I'm sure they're bound to listen to reason one of these days."

Christian poked a fork in his direction. "I know when I'm being mocked, but I also know I'm right, so I'll deal with it."

General Winter smiled. "Well, at least you have that going for you."

"Yes, my ability to withstand being harassed has come in handy more than once."

"I was referring to your willingness to entertain yourself, to have something you enjoy doing. Both of us know working in this office isn't the most leisurely of jobs, and you're required to do a great deal, and then you do double that. It's nice to hear you have something other than work."

That went a long way toward confirming Christian's steadfast belief that General Winter really and truly did care about the men and women who served under him. It was the same man who had tried and failed to get Christian to unload some of his work onto someone else, another assistant. It was also the same person who'd constantly given Christian hell about his chips and candy habit until, finally, Christian had given in and switched to veggies and fruits.

And to his great dismay, he enjoyed them.

"What about you? What do you do in your off time?" Christian asked.

"Crosswords."

Christian blinked. "Crosswords?"

General Winter laughed. "Yes, crosswords."

Christian narrowed his eyes. "You sit around in your quarters, doing crosswords the entire time?"

"Oh, yes. I have whole stacks of finished crosswords lining the shelves and tables of my home. It's got to the point that I could probably stuff the walls full of them and never have to worry about insulation."

Christian let out a heavy snort. "Okay, now I know you're being a smartass."

General Winter's eyes twinkled. "A little. Perhaps I enjoy giving you a taste of your own medicine."

"Bah! I'm not that bad."

Okay, so maybe he was fond of occasionally giving the

general a bit of a hard time. The man was so serious Christian found it nearly impossible to ignore the temptation. Plus, the fact that it brought a brief laugh or a flash of a smile to the general's face was more than enough to encourage him.

"I do enjoy crosswords, though," General Winter said.

"Just not enough to line the walls of your house."

"No."

"So, what *do* you like to do in your spare time?"

"This all relies on the fact that I have spare time to spend on anything."

Christian narrowed his eyes. "I get the feeling you're trying to avoid answering the question."

General Winter plucked a chip from his dish. "What do you think I enjoy doing?"

Christian let out a laugh, shaking his head. In truth, he had no idea. He could list, from memory, the general's measurements, what he did and didn't like with his food, his sleeping habits and workout schedule, and a whole host of other details that could be considered intimate. But when it came down to what General Winter might do in his spare time, Christian had no idea.

Christian decided to go with honesty. "I've worked for you for almost a year now, and honestly, I do not know what you do for fun."

General Winter leaned on the desk, chuckling. "Fair enough. It's not as if I knew you enjoyed coloring until only a few minutes ago."

Christian snorted. "I just got done thinking that despite everything about you, there are some things I just don't know."

General Winter nodded, taking another bite of his food and chewing thoughtfully. "How's your sister?"

"She's doing better. I haven't had a chance to call her yet, but we texted a bit yesterday. Apparently, she had a flare-up and had to take the day off. Nothing big."

"So, the medicine is working well for her then?"

"It's the first cluster she's had in months, and it didn't last days, so I'm going to say they are."

"A pity it doesn't get rid of them."

Christian smiled sadly. "The doctors were honest. They said there might be a chance the treatment wouldn't work at all or wouldn't have that much effect. Everyone reacts differently, and we were all kind of waiting with bated breath to see how it would go."

"Well, it's good the treatment is working. I know you were worried for a little while there," General Winter said.

Christian nodded. "Her and Lily are all I've had for years now. Mary's always been like my older sister, even when we got sent to different foster homes. Then she practically adopted Lily too. If it weren't for her, Lily would have had nowhere to go once she hit eighteen. I might not have either if I hadn't chosen to enlist."

"That why you enlisted, to make sure you had somewhere to stay?" General Winter asked with a slight crease in his brow.

"I wish I could say I signed up because I wanted to serve, to follow a higher calling or something. Some people joined and realized they'd found their home and that it was all they ever wanted. But really? Yeah, I joined because I knew I would have a constant source of income, a roof over my head, and food on the table."

General Winter wrinkled his nose. "I've heard that some of those homes can be...dire."

He shrugged. "Some were okay, some awful, but some were pretty great too. Don't get me wrong, there were people who were fostering so they could get a check and make themselves look like good people while spending the bare minimum on everyone to make sure they stayed alive. Nothing quite like being shoved four to a room, with food rationing like a third world dictatorship."

"It amazes me places like that still exist. It was one thing before the advent of stuff like the internet and cell phones, but now? So much has come out over the past few decades about how terrible some homes can be. Doesn't seem right that it continues," General Winter grumbled.

Christian laughed. "I mean, shit people are still going to be shit, and they're going to do shit things, even if the world is changing. Never really thought to look back, but I hope some of those homes are no longer taking in kids. Still, there were a lot of good ones."

"All things considered, it might not take much to be better than being half-starved by someone."

"True. But there was this older couple who lived off their pension and savings. It wasn't a lot, but they did a lot with what they had. The wife, Gloria, was a great gardener and cook. In the six months Lily and I were there, we learned how to keep the garden and preserve food, so stuff lasted for a long time."

"Oh, so that's where you met her?"

Christian nodded. "She showed up shortly after I did. She was as loud and pushy as she is now. There was no telling her no. Gloria adored her, though, loved her a 'girl with some spunk' or something like that. Her husband, Frank, was just as great. Despite years of working in a factory, he was an artist in his spare time. Used to let us kids watch him sketch and paint if we promised to be quiet, and even taught us some things. I was no good at it, but it got me into coloring."

"Really? I guess he left an impression on you."

"I also have a little window garden in my apartment. It's only growing a few herbs for cooking, but it's there."

"I stand corrected. They both left an impression on you."

Christian beamed. "They were wonderful people. They taught us how to take care of ourselves even if we don't have much, and they did it like the warmest and kindest people I've ever met. I like remembering those homes instead of all the miserable and cruel ones."

General Winter cocked his head, a small smile playing on his lips. "I think...that's a perfect way of looking at things."

Christian snorted. "Well, I like to think so. I thought the same thing growing up, but even the other kids used to say it was stupid. Now, as adults, most people look at me weirdly or say, 'how optimistic' but with that same tone, as if they're trying not to look at me like I'm a freak."

Most people assumed that someone who lost their parents at the age of nine and was thrown into a system that, even today, had plenty of pitfalls shouldn't be as cheerful as everyone said he was. Christian didn't understand why he couldn't see the good things in life and focus on them. There were plenty of good things in the world. You only had to keep your eye out for them.

"Reminds me of a quote I heard once, that it takes the same amount of energy to make yourself happy as it does to make yourself miserable, or something like that," General Winter said.

"Oh, I'm going to have to steal that one."

"By all means, I'm not sure I got it right. And for the record, I don't think there's anything wrong with keeping your attention on the positive. I think people are all too willing to look at the problems in the world, me included. And I think some of them forget that problems aren't what makes the world go round."

Christian nodded. "And the world needs people who focus on the problems; otherwise, we might not take them as seriously as we should."

"I think you're giving the pessimists too much credit."

"Maybe it's just because I'm naturally a happy-go-lucky person...apparently."

That brought a laugh from the general. "Fair enough. All the same, it's nice to have someone around here I can rely on to do their job well and also to be agreeable."

"Well, that's not the worst way someone has ever described me," Christian said with amusement.

General Winter winced, tapping the top of the desk. "Well...okay, that was a terrible compliment, wasn't it? I mean to say, if there were anyone I would choose to work alongside, knowing what I know now, I would choose you a thousand times over."

Christian had been joking when he'd commented on the general's compliment. Hearing an even better compliment from his lips left Christian with an open mouth and a still tongue. Color flooded his cheeks as he desperately tried to think of something to say that wouldn't sound like some cheesy soundbite and came up with nothing.

The only source of comfort from his embarrassment was that the general looked a little bashful. Anyone who didn't see him day in and day out might think General Winter was feeling grumpy or thinking a little too hard. Yet Christian had no other name for the creased brow and ever so slight pink on his cheek than embarrassment.

"I'm not even going to try to come back with anything because it's all going to sound stupid. So I'm just going to sit here and feel incredibly touched and thankful that I have someone like you to work under," Christian managed to say, proud that he didn't stutter over a single word.

General Winter continued to stare at him for what felt like forever. Christian found himself gazing into the pale green of the man's eyes for longer than he could ever remember doing before. For a moment, he watched the older man's lips twitch, and Christian's heart raced, wondering what was going to be said. He couldn't help but feel a slight twinge of disappointment when the general straightened instead, his features realigning to a dignified poise.

"Thank you, Christian, this has been a good lunch. Try to take advantage of the slow day and not work yourself to death," General Winter said as he retreated toward his office door.

"I make no promises," Christian called after him.

"I know."

It had been an odd moment. Christian couldn't say how he knew, but he'd been left with the impression that the general needed to say or do something rather than continue their staring match. Maybe the compliment shouldn't have affected him as much as it did, but Christian couldn't help basking in the warmth of a genuinely lovely comment as he turned his attention back to his work.

It wasn't until a few minutes later, as he was checking over the next day's schedule, that it occurred to him that General Winter had just...talked to him. It wasn't like they hadn't had conversations or passed different tidbits about one another casually across a room or desk. But it was the first time he could remember the two of them just having a one-on-one conversation. It left him feeling warm and wondering if the general was lonelier than he seemed.

Christian glanced at the small cloth doll that was supposed to be Lily. "I wouldn't mind being the one who kept him company a little more often."

Which was something he would never have dared to admit to his sister. She'd never let him live it down.

DAVID

Of all his job obligations, personally meeting with specially picked soldiers was one of his favorites. It allowed him to interact with the men and women who had their boots firmly on the ground and worked with the rest of the base. Part of it, he knew, was nostalgia. Seeing the younger generation as they learned to navigate the world was fascinating. It also didn't hurt that interacting with the younger military members allowed him to glimpse the changing ways of military life he might miss perched too high up.

Oscar Reyes was a good reminder of what David missed and what he was glad he avoided. An IED had taken half the man's arm and made his hip only half functional. As far as Command was concerned, Reyes would have been a better fit behind some desk for the rest of his career. Barring that, he might have been given early retirement with all the pretty commendations that meant shit to a soldier like Reyes.

Which was precisely what David tried to get across to the man after they'd made it through all the expected pleasantries. Reyes had listened raptly, his dark eyes searching

David's face constantly. Reyes waited until David finished his professional speech before replying.

"No offense, sir, but I'm sensing a 'but' somewhere in that explanation," Oscar said.

And therein lay the problem. He'd hoped to bring Oscar into the fold, placing him beneath Philip and inching him into the man's position. The problem was Philip was still being stubborn and dragging his heels.

David let out a slow breath, keeping his voice steady. "You would be correct. Currently, the position is occupied."

"Then, why am I here?"

Like he'd tell the man there was little more to the problem than politics. Soldiers like Reyes kept their heads down and away from the constant politicking and maneuvering that happened so often in the upper echelons of the military. David himself had been just like that when he'd been younger, and while he hadn't lost that attitude, necessity had forced him into the game all the same.

Damn it.

"Because once matters have settled, the position will become a vacancy," David promised.

The large man raised a brow as though expecting to hear something else. The truth was David wanted to lay the entire story out to him and let the man make an informed decision. The problem with politics was that David couldn't be sure he could trust everyone. While he had high hopes for the sort of person Reyes would be if he was given a chance to take Philip's place, David would have to wait before indulging the man's curiosity.

Oscar nodded. "Yes, sir. But that still doesn't tell me why I'm here now."

Direct. He liked that.

David nodded. "You're here now because there's no point wasting away at home or your family's home. While we're waiting for the vacancy to open up, I can easily find something for you to do. For the moment, I'm sure you can help out here in the office."

"Pure desk work," Oscar said, his voice tight with disdain.

He could remember the first time he'd been placed into an administrative capacity and how much he'd hated it. David had sworn up and down he would never be any good at pencil-pushing. Yet, despite that, he'd found a way to make it work. A good administrator in the military was a good leader, and a good leader could take the shittiest circumstances and make them work in their favor. Considering Reyes had already proven himself a capable field leader, David hoped he would find a way to navigate the safe, though not necessarily peaceful, deskwork.

General Winter chuckled. "You'll get used to it, and it's a perfect place to be if you're going to learn how things work around here. It'll give you a feel for working Stateside. We're a little less chaotic here."

"Not sure I know what to do without a bit of chaos," Oscar said.

"You'll find plenty. As much as we in the military like to make a big fuss about regimen and order, we're still people, and chaos follows in our wake. Perhaps by working at the center of it, you'll have a better idea of what you'll need to do once I can put you in your proper chair."

If there was anything he'd learned about juggling everything on the base, it was that he was never short of chaos and confusion. Everywhere he looked, something demanded his attention or his direct intervention. Maybe with Reyes eventually at the helm of Operations, David might be able to take a breath.

To his relief, Oscar let out a sigh and gave a nod. "Yes, sir. When do I begin?"

"You can start in a few days. Give yourself a chance to look around first and rest after moving across the country."

"Yes, sir," Oscar said.

David smiled, checking his screen. "Ah, right, and just as a formality, do me a favor and report to the clinic on base as well. I require all newcomers to go in for a check-up, no matter how recent their last examination was."

"Yes, sir," Oscar said with a curt nod.

It was as good a time as any to end the conversation. Reyes had been dragged across the country and was expected to settle in quickly. Having been the one to order that and follow it up with unsettling news, David felt he owed the man a break.

David stood. "Then I think that about covers everything. You'll have a couple of days to find your feet, maybe see the sights a little. But I'll need you in here on Monday at 0700, got it?"

Oscar stood, snapping a salute. "Yes, sir."

David motioned toward the door. "Dismissed."

With that, Reyes walked out, a noticeable limp in his step. David stared at the door thoughtfully, hoping he wasn't pushing things too far. Philip had enough sway with Command through his connections that David was already pushing his luck trying to move the man to another position. Reyes had only recovered from his injuries over the last few months, and there was no telling what his mental state was like after being half-blown to hell. If David's decision blew up in his face, Reyes might pay a higher price than everyone else.

"Hell," David muttered.

His door opened, and Christian walked in, frowning down at a tablet. "Why am I expected to order some fancy keyboard and have it here and ready to use on Monday?"

David eyed him. "Normally, people warn me before they walk into my office."

Christian looked up. "And why is it being delivered to this office instead of somewhere else?"

David sighed. "Because you're getting an assistant."

Christian narrowed his eyes. "I told you, I don't need the help."

Yes, he had, several times as far as David could remember. Honestly, with how quick Christian was to refuse help and how adamantly he'd been sticking to it, David wondered if he hadn't struck a nerve by suggesting it.

"Well, good for us both because this isn't necessarily about helping you. It's about helping the man who just left my office and me," David told him.

"No offense, but how does my getting an assistant help you?" Christian asked, a wounded note in his voice.

David smiled. "You're doing the work of three people, and then some probably. Trust me, this isn't because you're not doing your job well."

"I wasn't thinking that," Christian said, though the relief in his eyes betrayed his thoughts.

David pointed to the door, "Close that if you would."

Christian did so. "What's going on?"

"I hope to place Reyes directly under Philip...as a second in command. It will give him a good feel for the job, and more likely than not, Philip will pass a great deal onto Reyes."

"Which makes him look bad and Reyes better."

David winced. "I don't want...to ruin Philip's career or have him demoted. There are plenty of positions somewhere else that would suit him far better. And I firmly believe Reyes has the potential to perform the role quite well."

"So, not so much ruin him, but make Reyes look better."

David nodded. "If I wanted to ruin Philip, I could. But this isn't about that, and never was."

"Wait, what dirt do you have on Philip?"

David blinked, realizing he'd let information slip. Damn, what was it about Christian that drove David to forget himself so easily?

"Don't worry about that. That's between Philip and me."

Christian huffed. "Well, that's no fun. You can't tease me with some delicious tidbit and leave it a mystery."

"I can when I shouldn't have said anything to begin with."

Christian continued to stare at him with a frown. David would never admit it, but he honestly couldn't take the frown seriously. Something was endearing about his subordinate, a man over twenty years his junior, trying to stare him down. As much as he knew it would ruin Christian's attempts if David called it cute, there was no way he was saying it.

Christian sighed, giving up. "Alright, so what am I supposed to do?"

"Order the keyboard for him and have it here overnight so you can look it over. After that, get him going with his setup and teach him how to do your job."

"And how does that help?"

"It gives him something to do, which he's been without since he woke up in a hospital months ago. It also gives us time to allow Philip to stop being so stubborn about having someone else in his office with him."

Christian raised a brow, smirking. "Us, huh?"

David frowned. "What?"

"You said us, not you."

David blinked. "Well, I suppose I did. You are apparently included because you casually brought yourself into this little mess."

And unlike Reyes, who was an unknown, David trusted Christian.

Christian smiled. "I take it the keyboard is for Oscar."

"Yes. I looked into it, and this one came highly recommended. I doubt you'll need to learn much, as it'll mostly be him who needs to use it. However, it wouldn't hurt you to ensure it works and everything is ready for him. I'm having him come in at 0700 on Monday."

"I really hope this isn't your way of trying to drive the man crazy. If you had any idea what kind of shit comes through that elevator half the time, you might rethink putting someone else out there."

David chuckled, opening his messages again. "I'm sure Reyes will be just fine. He's dealt with his fair share, and you'll be there to guide him. If anyone can make sure he finds his feet and can handle whatever madness this place can throw, it'll be you."

Christian hummed. "Not sure if that's a compliment or a criticism."

"It was meant to be a compliment, but the more I think about it, the more it begs the question as to whether you're completely sane," David said with a small smile.

"Right, so a compliment," Christian said.

"Yes, I suppose it would have to be, wouldn't it?"

"Keep complimenting me, general, and I might start to like it," Christian said as he returned to the waiting room.

David looked up from his computer, blinking at the closed door. Had that been...no, it couldn't have been. David would not entertain the idea that Christian had come even remotely close to flirting with him, no matter how tempting the idea was. Hell, the fact that it *was* tempting was a clear indicator that he needed to keep his attention on his work.

He turned back to the screen and stopped at the newest message. It simply said, 'Read this.' David could see an attachment, and he debated whether or not to open the message in the first place. After another moment of hesitation, he opened it and saw the attachment was a video.

Attached was a short message.

If you don't want people seeing this, you should call me.
E

David could not think of a time when he'd felt confusion and foreboding as he read the cryptic message. What in all hell was happening? He was obviously being threatened, but by who? All he had was a letter, and as he stared at the attachment, he thought he might figure it out quickly.

Taking a deep breath, he clicked the link and opened it. The program popped up on the screen, showing it was a full two minutes. David didn't take long to realize what he was seeing, and he felt his stomach plummet.

Now he knew who 'E' was. Jesus, it had been months since he'd last seen Ethan. The younger man had worked at a cocktail bar David had gone to for a meeting with another general. Glances had been exchanged, and then Ethan had slipped David his number. They enjoyed one another for a few weeks after that. Despite his stamina, David had more often than not found himself worn out by Ethan's exuberance and determination.

But it had been short-lived, something David had been honest about from the start. Ethan was cute and fun, but that was all it could ever be. Despite liking younger men, he rarely found himself emotionally attracted to them. Men in their early twenties were generally good-looking, rowdy, and fun to roll around in bed with. However, they still had years of life experience to attain before David found himself genuinely interested. Ethan still had a lot of growing up to do, and when the excitement had worn off, David had parted ways, just as he'd warned the man would inevitably happen.

And Ethan had promised he'd deleted the video.

"Apparently not," David muttered as he watched himself on the screen.

His phone buzzed, pulling him out of his horrified stillness with a jerk. He stared at the device as if he'd never seen it before, stiffening when he saw an unknown number on the screen.

He answered it. "Hello?"

"Good, you answered."

David tightened his jaw. "Ethan."

"You read the message, right? You didn't just watch us having a bit of fun."

David glanced toward the office door. "How did you even know I saw the damn thing?"

"You know you can get a notification if someone reads your message, right?"

Right.

"Fine, you have my attention now what do you want?"

"Look, you've seen enough movies and shit, right? You know how this goes."

David made an ugly face. "Money?"

It wasn't like he was going to pretend to be surprised, but it just seemed so...predictable.

David pinched his brow. "How much?"

"You know what? I've been thinking about that for a while, and I'm having a hard time coming up with a good number. But you know, you've got to have some money. I mean, big-time general like you, you should have plenty of money."

He didn't make quite as much as Ethan apparently thought. True, he probably made enough to be the envy of a cocktail server at an upscale bar, but it didn't make him rich. Considering he spent most of his time working, his budget was mostly spent on food and little else. His savings were considerable, but he'd never thought they might have to be put to *this* use.

David gritted his teeth. "How the hell am I supposed to come up with the correct amount?"

"You're a smart man, David. I'm sure you can figure out

how much is enough to keep this video from getting to the wrong eyes. I mean, hell, it's the 2010s, right? Being with a guy isn't *that* big a deal...maybe. But having a bit of fun with someone young enough to be your son? Shit, I bet the internet would *love* that," Ethan said with far more relish than David would have preferred.

"I don't have much of a choice, do I?"

"Not really, no."

"Fine, then just...why?"

"Why?"

"Yes. Why are you doing this?"

"You break my heart, I break your bank...or your reputation, that's up to you."

David jerked back from the phone in surprise. "What? I told you from the beginning there was an expiration date for whatever we had going on. I told you I was only in it to enjoy what we could enjoy, and then we'd move on. You had the choice to walk away, and you chose to keep going."

"And I wanted more."

The fact that he'd agreed to David's terms obviously meant nothing. David could only stare at the phone in utter disbelief as the reality of the situation settled into his gut. Was he really being blackmailed by a man who should have been nothing more than a fond memory because he'd walked away after saying he would?

Hell, he'd stepped in it, hadn't he?

David closed his eyes, knowing he had no choice but to ask, "How long do I have?"

"Tell you what, I'm feeling nice since you're probably going to be so generous, ya know? So how about I give you the weekend. Monday at this time, and you tell me your offer."

"And if you like it?"

"You give me the money, and I give you the USB stick it's on."

David blinked. "You...keep it on a memory drive?"

"I'm not giving you my computer. You'll get the original copy on a drive when I get the money."

"The money I have to figure out."

"You figure out the price of your long-served career."

David closed his eyes. "Fine."

"I'll call you on Monday."

The line clicked off, leaving David to stare at his phone in helpless horror.

CHRISTIAN

Saturdays were not Christian's favorite day working in the office. It was when reports of whatever the soldiers got up to the night before came rolling in. Christian's Saturday morning was typically spent on the phone, fielding calls from the nearby town and people on base with complaints and reminders.

Honestly, only so much could be done when a soldier got a little too drunk and feisty. The military police worked hard to keep everything on base peaceful, though some days were harder than others. For those that created trouble in town, it was up to the regular police. Of course, if the soldiers got into trouble with the law, they were in for a whole lot of hell when they came back to base.

Not that it stopped the calls, though, much to Christian's irritation.

Christian rubbed his brow. "Look, Chief Williams, I understand, truly, I do. I'll pass the message along to General Winter, and I'm sure he will speak with...Private Jonas' superior officer."

The police chief growled. "That's what you always say, and nothing ever changes."

Christian rolled his eyes. "Save for locking the men down every weekend and preventing them from leaving the base, which is not policy or law, we cannot do much. We can, however, promise the private in question will be reprimanded once he has been released from your custody."

"Oh, he's already out. Drunk tank for the night, but he might be looking at some battery charges and destruction of property."

Christian grimaced, wonderful. "Well, keep us updated. Either way, Private Jonas will probably wish you'd kept him in jail a little longer after his CO is done with him."

Who gave the police chief the phone number for General Winter's office? Christian was going to strangle them.

"Fine. But I'm growing tired of the General avoiding speaking to me directly. This is the fourth time in two weeks."

"I understand that, but the general has a lot on his plate."

Not only that, but Christian had noticed a change in the general over the past couple of days. Christian had no idea what had happened, but General Winter's ordinarily quiet and serious nature had become downright surly and almost mute. Christian had received a grunt that morning when he'd greeted him, which was out of character. General Winter was not a talkative man, but he wasn't rude.

"Apparently so busy he can't make time to speak to the chief of police," Chief Williams grumbled.

"No offense meant, but General Winter has very little time for things that aren't absolutely pressing."

"Right, and his men causing trouble in *my* city doesn't warrant his attention."

Christian narrowed his eyes. "How many drunk and

disorderly people do you pick up on a Friday night, Chief Williams? How many people do you arrest for battery?"

"Pardon?"

"How many of them are for domestic assault? Rape? Attempted murder, or even murder?"

"What does that have to do with anything?"

Christian reached out, opening a message as it popped up on his screen. "I want you to take the number of people you arrest on a weekend for all those things and combine them. Then, I want you to pick out the ones done by the soldiers from our base. Can you do that for me?"

"I can't say I have the exact numbers right in front of me," Chief Williams said tightly.

"No, probably not, but I'm sure you have a good idea that if we compared the numbers, you'd find a big difference between the number of people arrested from the city or are tourists and those that come off this base. So yes, the general is a little too busy to deal with a statistical minority personally."

There was a pause before Chief Williams recovered himself. "You little shit."

Christian shook his head. "I think that marks the end of this conversation. I'll deliver the message to General Winter. Have a nice day."

The police chief continued speaking angrily. Still, Christian ended the call without bothering to listen to more. No doubt, the police chief would soon realize he'd been hung up on and would call back.

"Sucks for him since I'm the one answering the damn phone," Christian muttered.

"Who did you piss off?"

General Winter's voice from behind brought Christian around with a slight yelp. He was standing outside his office door, frowning at Christian.

"Jesus, sir, you scared the hell out of me," Christian complained, holding a hand to his beating chest.

He hated it when the general snuck up on him like that.

"I'm putting a damn bell on that door," Christian continued.

"You didn't answer my question."

Christian was again struck by the strange mood. Christian wanted to ask what was wrong but didn't know how. For all their comfort with one another and ease of conversation, there was still that gap between them.

Christian glanced at the phone nervously. "Ah, the police chief?"

"What did he want?"

"Apparently, another private got himself in trouble last night and was thrown in the drunk tank."

"And? People have been getting drunk and doing stupid things since alcohol was invented. Why is that my problem?"

Christian raised a brow. "As I've mentioned before, Chief Williams gets testy when it happens a few too many times for his liking. Though I probably didn't help by pointing out that compared to how many people arrested who don't come from here, our soldiers are pretty well behaved."

"Good. Maybe that will give him something to think about for a while. I'll speak to him some other time and remind him he has more important things to do than to waste our time."

Christian squirmed, pleased he wasn't going to get his ass reamed but still uncomfortable with the irritation in the general's voice. It wasn't like General Winter to express aggravation. One of Christian's favorite things about working for General Winter, besides his genuine care for his men, was that he seemed to draw from an infinite well of patience. Seeing him irritable was surreal.

"Uh, sir?"

"Yes?"

Christian tried to hold the other man's gaze. "Is everything okay?"

General Winter frowned. "I'm fine, why?"

"Because you don't seem...fine."

"Really?"

Christian grinned nervously. "Yeah, really. I know I talked about how there are things I don't know about you, things that are weird not to know when I think about it, but...I know what you're like day to day. And you're...off. You've been off the past couple of days."

General Winter blinked at him. "Oh. My apologies."

"Something wrong?"

General Winter shook his head, the surprise disappearing behind an impassive expression. Christian was almost impressed with how quickly the older man locked his emotions behind a professional mask.

"No. Just a few things on my mind. It will pass. I haven't been sleeping too well, and I think I might take the next hour to myself. Maybe have a little nap."

"In your office?"

"Yes, can you adjust my meetings today?"

"I can do that, yeah."

"Thank you."

Christian watched him walk stiffly into his office and continued to stare after him. Since when did General Winter, the workaholic who barely knew the meaning of a proper night's sleep, take a nap in the middle of the day? The thought was even more troubling than knowing something was bothering the general. It was one thing for him to be worried, but for it to coincide with uncharacteristic exhaustion?

"What the hell?" Christian muttered, turning back to his computer.

Fixing the schedule to put everything back an hour was no big deal. Christian's Saturday might be packed for the first half, but General Winter normally had an easier day. It was nothing to move things around and reschedule the medic's visit for Monday.

Yet the ease of his work also meant he could ponder what was wrong with the general. On some level, he figured he shouldn't be bothered. Everyone had their off days, after all, and sometimes that went on for more than a day. And it wasn't like the general was a young man. For all Christian knew, General Winter could be in pain, or just slowing down.

Christian wrinkled his nose. "Nah."

Okay, sure, the man wasn't getting any younger, but a person didn't just start to run into the ground overnight. If the general had started to slow down due to age, Christian would have seen the signs long before now. Plus, he made sure the general saw the medics just as often as he insisted the other soldiers on the base did. Christian wasn't supposed to know the results of those exams, but he had an understanding with the clinic that if there was anything he needed to know to keep the general healthy, it should be passed along quietly.

"Dammit, Christian. Don't do this to yourself. Just...focus on something else," Christian chided himself.

That something was combing through the message system. If there was one thing Christian was not the best at keeping up with, it was purging messages. When he was responsible for both his message box and that of the general, it could fill up pretty quickly if he wasn't diligent. Most of the time, though, it ended up being hundreds of messages in each box that he had to go through and delete, save, or mark for later consideration.

However, it did the job of refocusing his mind. Christian's

inbox had been the first on his list, and he was dismayed to find several hundred messages waiting. Most of the time, it just required a brief look, but some required him to read the contents. The task took almost an hour, and it kept his thoughts from his worries.

"Done is done," Christian proclaimed proudly as he closed his inbox.

Then again, there was still the general's inbox.

Sighing, he opened it and began combing through it. Opening the first message, he scanned its contents before deciding it wasn't needed. His decision to throw it in the trash folder stopped him in his tracks when he realized there was already something in the folder. It honestly didn't matter if he was the one who read it or the general, it would always be Christian who inevitably decided to delete emails. General Winter left the decision of what to keep and what to get rid of up to Christian, if only because there might be something in the messages that Christian might need.

But Christian hadn't cleared the old messages in quite a while.

"Dammit, general," he muttered as he opened the folder.

He stopped, raising a brow at the demanding title. Opening it brought his other brow up.

"Don't want people to see this?" Christian read aloud.

There was an attachment, a video file from the looks of it. Christian's heart pounded as he hovered the cursor over the link, pondering what to do. On the one hand, it was clearly not meant for his eyes. On the other, there was obviously something very wrong with this message, and he wasn't sure he could leave well enough alone when it looked like someone was threatening the general.

He clicked it.

It took the computer a couple of minutes to download the

file. A two-minute-long video popped up on the built-in player.

"All that for two minutes? Must be HD," Christian muttered, clicking the play button.

And immediately froze.

The first few seconds of the movie were taken from the perspective of someone lying on their back. A bedroom could be seen in the background, with pants thrown over a desk chair, a laptop, and a closet. Far more interesting to Christian was the very naked man who stood in the center of the shot.

General Winter.

The camera stayed panned up, just low enough that Christian could see it didn't look like the salt in the general's hair had crept to his groin yet. Amidst the utter shock of what he was seeing, some part of Christian's brain couldn't help but think the general was in *very* good shape for someone closer to fifty than forty. In the sunlight coming from somewhere behind the camera, Christian could see just about every detail of the general's body from the waist up. His body was still tight with muscle, though perhaps it didn't have the definition of a younger man. Sparse hair trailed down the general's flat stomach and up to his chest. His arms looked even more impressive out of his uniform, and Christian's breath stuttered as he watched the muscles shift and flex.

He was never happier that he'd long ago muted the sound from the computer after being irritated half to death by the message alert noise. Christian watched as the general bent down, a wicked smile on his face as he ran his hands up the pair of legs of the person filming. Christian didn't need the camera to pan down to show the filmer's straining, eager cock, or to know that the person being stroked by General Winter was a man.

Well, that certainly settled whether or not the general was into men.

Christian sat frozen with a mixture of complete shock and growing arousal as the video continued to play to the end. He watched as the general, his boss, a man he'd nursed a quiet attraction to for almost a year, worked his way up the filmer's body. Light kisses were laid upon the other man's skin, trailing up the man's inner thighs to his hips. The camera shook a little as the general's mouth continued to wander, taking his time as he explored the other man's body.

The clip finally ended with the general's face in full view. Christian sat there, staring at the image, transfixed by the sight of General Winter's expression. Of all the emotions he'd seen on the other man's face, Christian had never seen pure arousal before. Lust practically radiated from General Winter's eyes as he stayed locked in the screen. And while it wasn't actually aimed at Christian, he couldn't help but feel the effect of the expression.

Slowly recovering his composure, he cleared his throat and forced his eyes away from the image. His uniform pants were uncomfortably tight, and Christian did not want to continue staring. Though he hadn't seen everything, and it was obvious the clip was part of a longer video, Christian knew damn well he was going to be adding that to his memory banks for later use.

When his eyes settled back on the screen, he tried to avoid the small window where the stilled video sat. Instead, Christian looked at the email behind the video and read what was there again. Though it was apparent the email was threatening, he couldn't understand its point. Obviously, someone wanted something from General Winter and was using the video as leverage.

Would it matter if someone saw the video? As far as Christian knew, the general wasn't married and hadn't seen anyone seriously in the past year. How could a sex tape be used against him? And what exactly did this person want?

"And who is it?" Christian wondered, his mind now transfixed on the mystery.

The person he couldn't see in the video? Looking at the properties of the video didn't add much information, citing the date as a few days ago. That didn't mean much when the clip was obviously taken from a longer video and would have been created recently. Was it a former lover, spurned by something the man did and seeking revenge? Or was it just blackmail?

"What the hell are you doing?"

The general's voice sent an icepick into Christian's chest, and he froze. His mind flashed back to when he had chided the general for being so quiet earlier and the man's comment about taking a brief rest. Closing his eyes, Christian turned to face the office door.

"Hi, General Winter."

DAVID

Fighting to maintain his self-control, David repeated his question. "What the hell are you doing?"

David had read about people looking like they wanted to disappear on the spot, but he didn't think he'd ever seen it in real life. Christian physically cringed, leaning back and hunching his shoulders until his neck almost disappeared. Guilt was written in every inch of the wince on his face.

"I…" Christian began, mouth working silently.

David's eyes leaped back to the computer screen, and his mouth became an even thinner line. That damned video, which had haunted him ever since he'd seen it the other day, was sitting in the video player. From a few feet away, David could see the video had played through to the end and Ethan's message attached to it.

Christian recovered enough to begin speaking rapidly. "I was going through the emails and purging them. I did mine first, and when I started on yours, I saw a message in the trash. You don't get rid of stuff, so I opened it to see what was going on."

David cursed inwardly. He wasn't surprised it had

attracted Christian's attention. The man was incredibly attentive to detail and naturally curious. David could remember all too well the times he'd found Christian looking around his office, peering at everything as if needing to absorb every detail. Then there were the times he'd found Christian reading files, albeit not classified, just because they were interesting.

The entire blackmail attempt had thrown him off, and he hadn't deleted the email.

"And you just decided to watch the video?" David asked.

Christian's fingers danced nervously on his armrest. "Well, I read the message, saw the attachment, clicked it, and then just—"

David waited before asking, "Just what?"

Christian's face reddened. "Found myself staring. I couldn't—"

David narrowed his eyes, darting all over Christian's flushed features. The other man had been staring?

"Enjoy the show?" David asked curtly.

"Uh—"

It had been meant as a smart-ass comment, but now it was David's turn to find himself unsure what to say.

Christian winced. "Uh, you look good?"

David blinked. "You...were enjoying it?"

Christian's eyes widened, waving his hands frantically. "I wasn't watching it because I was trying to enjoy myself. I just...wasn't expecting what I saw. Kind of just froze and couldn't look away."

"But...look good?" David asked in disbelief.

Christian sputtered, hands flopping uselessly. "I have no idea what to say right now, that isn't going to make things worse."

As if it wasn't bad enough that some crazed former lover was blackmailing David, now Christian had seen the evidence. What the hell was David supposed to do now? And much to his confusion, some part of him thrilled knowing Christian had not only seen it but apparently enjoyed it.

Christian looked down at his hands, fidgeting with his fingers. The pained expression on his face brought a stab of guilt to David's angry thoughts, and he felt himself deflate. Christian was given a great deal of latitude in his job, and it wasn't the first time he'd accidentally stumbled across something he wasn't supposed to see. Of course, every instance before hadn't been quite as mortifying for either of them.

David sighed. "Come into my office."

Christian winced again but stood up with a nod. David turned and walked into his office, rubbing his forehead as he tried to figure out what he was going to do. He'd spent the better part of the last couple of days trying to figure it out. Now, there was one more wrinkle to smooth.

David motioned to one of the two comfortable chairs across from his desk. "Take a seat."

Not bothering to see if Christian listened, David went to the cabinet at the back of the room. It was filled with bottles of expensive alcohol meant for special guests. David wasn't one for drinking when he was working, or at all for the most part, but he thought he could make an exception this time.

"And to think, I never actually took that nap. I spent most of that hour by myself wondering what I was going to do," David said as he opened the cabinet.

"I am sorry," Christian said quietly.

"Yes, I know."

And he did. Despite his frustration, David knew Christian would never mean any harm. Despite the professional distance enforced on them by their jobs, David knew Christian well enough to count him among the few people he could trust. Christian had spent the past year doing his job with a passion and dedication David appreciated and respected. Despite his curious and often intrusive nature, Christian had never done anything he knew would violate David's trust.

Deciding on a smooth whiskey with a slight bite, David pulled out two glasses. He pulled out the tiny bucket of ice cubes from the small fridge and dropped a few into each glass.

David thought about it, added another measure to each glass, and held one out to Christian. The blond looked at the glass as though he'd never seen one before, requiring David to give it a slight shake for emphasis. Christian took it, looked at it again, and then drank. David smiled when Christian's eyes widened, staring at the glass with wonder.

"Good?" David asked.

"What the hell is it?"

"Whiskey?"

Christian looked up, wide-eyed still. "I *hate* whiskey."

David snorted, setting the bottle down and taking up his glass. "No, you hate cheap whiskey. I've yet to meet anyone who's disliked this. Which is good because it's a few hundred dollars a bottle."

Christian looked at his glass, blanching. "Jesus. You're telling me I'm drinking more than my lunch cost?"

"Probably."

"God, it's good, though."

David nodded, taking his seat. "Be careful. It can sneak up on you."

"I'll keep that in mind."

They settled into silence, staring at their glasses. David evaluated his thoughts and found he wasn't as angry as he might have been. Christian had been ready to shrink into himself and disappear, and David didn't think that was just because he'd been caught. The last thing David wanted was to punish Christian over what amounted to an accident.

"You're being threatened?" Christian finally asked.

David looked up, sighing. "Yes."

"By who?"

Well, the cat was already halfway out of the bag. There didn't seem to be much harm in letting it out the rest of the way. And perhaps Christian might be able to give him an idea of what David could do. Another perspective might help, even if it was just to pick a dollar amount and hope it was enough.

"A former lover of mine."

Christian winced. "I thought that was the case. The guy in the video?"

"Yes."

"I take it things didn't end well, huh?"

David shook his head. "That's the problem. I thought it ended perfectly amicably. It was...never meant to be serious."

Christian smiled softly. "So, a fuck buddy."

David wrinkled his nose. "For lack of a better word, yes, I suppose."

Christian covered his mouth, prompting David to ask what was wrong.

"It's just you were willing to sleep with the guy, have a sexual relationship, and let him film it, but you're being stuffy about calling him a fuck buddy."

"I just don't like the term."

"I can see that."

David frowned. "And in my defense, he assured me he'd deleted it well before we ended things."

Christian shook his head. "Take it from me, most people are not going to delete something like that. They'll keep it for their own use later. Though I don't like the idea that some of them are keeping it for something like this."

David cocked his head. "Have you?"

"Have I what?"

"Kept something like that?"

"A sex tape?"

David shrugged. "From one of your previous...uh, lovers."

Christian grinned. "I've never made a sex tape with any of my *boyfriends*, if that's what you're asking."

Well, it certainly covered everything David had been asking. In truth, David had never been sure where Christian leaned. He suspected he was into men, but there had been no obvious clues. Christian always kept private information about his dating life utterly non-existent in the office, and David couldn't recall a time he had ever seen the man looking at anyone with interest.

"Why not?" David asked.

Christian shrugged. "I've never trusted anyone enough to take that kind of film of me, and I've never wanted to do it with anyone before, either. Not that it couldn't be fun because I'm sure it could be."

"Right up until they come back around and blackmail you for money."

"Oh, Jesus. Of course it's money."

David couldn't help his laugh. "I had much the same thought when he told me."

"So, who's he? Like, his name."

"His name is Ethan. I met him at a cocktail bar a handful of months back."

Christian cocked his head, hand sliding to his pocket. "Which one?"

"Diamond Den."

Christian nodded. "I know who you're talking about."

David straightened. "A friend of yours?"

Christian shook his head. "No, but he's on one of those dating apps. Has his name up and lists himself as working there. I've seen him online quite a bit. Didn't know you went for the younger ones, General."

David wrinkled his nose again. "And you weren't supposed to know. No one was supposed to know about that save for the few people I enjoyed private time with."

"Sorry, just trying to lighten the mood a little."

"I know, but I'm having a hard time finding the lighter side of things at the moment."

"Yeah, I can understand that."

David watched Christian as he mulled over the information. He couldn't help but wonder, considering what he'd just confirmed about Christian's tastes, if the younger man had got some enjoyment out of the video. David wasn't thrilled that someone else was in on the entire disaster, but he'd be lying if he said some part of him, a decidedly horny part, wanted to know what Christian thought of what he'd seen.

And what it would have looked like if Christian had been the one holding the camera that night.

Stirring, David shifted in his seat. "In any case. He contacted me the other day through that message and apparently had it set up to alert him when the email was opened. He then called me and let me know what he wanted."

"How much?"

David shook his head. "Ethan has decided to play games. Rather than tell me what he wants, he's making me decide how much my career is worth."

"Wow, that's...evil."

"Yes, apparently, he likes to play with his food."

"Have you considered going to the police? Blackmail is illegal."

David sighed, draining the last of the whiskey before continuing. "I have, as I'm sure anyone being blackmailed would. The problem is it wouldn't stop him from simply releasing the video onto the internet anyway. At that point, what would he have to lose?"

Christian fiddled with his glass. "I mean...would it be that bad? We're well past the point of anyone caring about the whole being with other guys thing, right?"

David smiled ruefully. "If it were just a matter of being with another man, it wouldn't be a problem. That it was with someone who was nineteen and allowed to be filmed...well."

"There are people who get with people who are eighteen. What does it matter?"

"To you and me, nothing. But to Command? It wouldn't look good if a high-ranking general had random flings with men half their age. It wouldn't necessarily ruin my reputation, but it would certainly look bad. I imagine I would find myself quietly, slowly, but inevitably, brought down from my position and filed off somewhere else."

Christian frowned. "You're telling me just because you're with another guy, a young guy, you'd be shoved into a corner to be forgotten about?"

"If it were a relationship, and not a casual relationship of a strictly sexual nature, one that allowed for filming, probably not. I would be spoken of, but considering this is behavior that would be considered unbecoming of a man of my station, I would find myself in a lot of trouble, albeit the hidden kind."

Christian snorted. "How stupid."

"That's just how it goes."

"So now you're stuck either letting this happen and letting him get whatever money you can come up with or risk everything you've worked for?"

"That more or less sums up my problem, yes."

Christian huffed. "Well, that explains why you've been in such a mood."

David frowned. "A mood? Yes, I imagine I have been. This has been weighing on my mind quite heavily."

"I like you better when you're trying not to laugh at my smart-ass jokes."

"And I prefer trying not to laugh at your jokes."

"So, what are you going to do?"

Now, there was the question. David had been thinking long and hard about what amount of money would satisfy Ethan and guarantee an end to the entire thing. He still had another day and a half to give it some thought, but he could feel time ticking away rapidly.

David laughed humorlessly. "How much do you think would be a good amount to offer him? I don't want to lose my entire savings over this, but I don't want to risk insulting him either."

Christian snorted. "It sounds like he could use a bit of insulting."

"Yes, but I won't be the one to do it."

"No, I bet you wouldn't."

"So, now you know everything I know, what would you offer?"

"If I had my way, you wouldn't pay a cent," Christian grumbled.

"Trust me, if I could think of a way to get out of this mess without ruining everything, I'd take it in a heartbeat. But considering he doesn't seem willing to negotiate outside his demands, talking to him isn't an option."

Christian cocked his head thoughtfully. "True. I imagine you're the last person he's going to want to deal with."

"Hell, he's so paranoid about what I could do. He thinks I could...summon someone to access his information, get into his online storage, and take the file down."

Christian frowned. "It is possible."

"You know how?"

"Uh, no, not personally. I'm good with computers, but not that good. I have...uh, friends."

"Friends who can hack into people's computers."

"Look, some people in the foster system don't come out

law-abiding people like me. I'm not saying they've told me what they do, but I can guess."

"And since you don't have any proof—"

"Then, I don't know anything, right."

"That's fair."

Christian pulled his phone out, looking at the screen. "If he doesn't have it stored digitally, he just...has it on a computer?"

"Yes. He said he'd put it on a thumb drive."

"And how do you know he won't keep a copy to come around again?"

David sighed, heart sinking. "I don't."

Christian frowned thoughtfully, opening something on his phone and flipping around momentarily. David watched, wondering what the younger man could be doing as Christian started typing. The phone buzzed a moment later, bringing a smirk to Christian's face.

David eyed him warily. "What?"

"I have an idea, that's what."

David would usually be pleased to hear Christian had an idea. However, considering the circumstances, he could feel himself growing cautious. Christian was a good man and far more mature at twenty-five than David remembered being. That did not, however, prevent Christian from being a little impulsive.

"And does this idea involve something foolish that could worsen this situation?" David asked.

Christian looked up, thoughtful. "Well...no, I don't think it would make it worse. I'm pretty sure it's completely safe for you."

"Okay, and are you planning on sharing your idea?"

"Mm, no."

"No?"

"No."

"Why not?"

Christian laughed, standing up. "Because if I told you, my plan probably wouldn't work. So here's the thing, I'm going to take the rest of the night off and tomorrow. When are you supposed to contact him?"

"He's going to call me Monday afternoon."

"Good, that works perfectly. Don't bother responding to anything he sends, and I'll see you Monday morning," Christian said, making for the door.

David stood up, holding a hand out. "Now, hold on a minute."

Christian turned, winking. "Look, you trust me, right?"

"With a lot of things, yes, but this is a very different set of circumstances."

Christian smiled gently. "Look, I know this is a...well, a fucked-up situation. And I know I'm probably not the first person you would have turned to for help, but I promise you, I have a great idea and know what I'm doing. And even if it doesn't work, I'll ensure it doesn't make things worse, okay?"

Christian's voice had a note of pleading, and David felt his protest die in his throat. Everything he'd said was true, but David still couldn't help the apprehension as he nodded, sitting down to let Christian leave the office without further protest.

Damn him for being a sucker for a cute face.

CHRISTIAN

The bar wasn't busy on a Sunday night, and Christian wasn't sure if he should consider it a blessing or a curse. It made it easy to look around the crowd as he walked through double doors. The bar, equipped with only one bartender, had a line of stools. To Christian's right was a dance floor with two platforms with dance poles. There wasn't a single person on the dance floor, let alone the poles, he noticed with faint amusement.

To the left, booths and tables lined the floor. A couple of the booths were occupied already, so he turned his attention away. Christian checked his messages again, confirming he was in the right place. The sign said Coco's outside, though Christian thought that was a pretty energetic name for a place with maybe a dozen people.

Rereading the message, he looked, finding another area behind the bar. Waving to the frowning bartender, he mounted the steps to the semi-enclosed space. There was only one person sitting at one of the booths, and he matched the picture Christian had been looking at on the dating app.

"Ethan?" Christian asked hesitantly as he approached the man.

"That's me," Ethan said with a grin.

Christian had to give General Winter that much, Ethan *was* a good-looking man. He was a couple of inches shorter than Christian, which would have made him over half a foot shorter than the general. Ethan's hair and eyes were light brown, which, with his tanned skin, made him look like a native of the tropical climate. He was on the slight side, but it was obvious he didn't neglect his body, as the arms showing through the muscle shirt were well-toned. His features were slightly angular, giving the man 'elfin' features. He showed gracefulness, which became apparent as he exited the booth to greet Christian.

Christian chuckled. "I guess I should have known. There's not exactly a lot of people in here. It wouldn't have been too hard to find you."

"Well, and I hope my pictures managed to do me *some* justice," Ethan said.

Christian grinned at the subtle show of confidence. "Alright, well, you have me there."

Ethan gestured toward the bar. "You want something to drink?"

"Hm, I don't know what they have here."

"Not a whole lot, or rather, not that great. But I like meeting people here since it's quiet."

"I suppose we could have a drink or two," Christian said.

Ethan chuckled. "In a rush to get out of here?"

Christian shrugged, putting on a mock air of coyness. "I guess you could say I've enjoyed what I've seen so far."

"Man, I must be charming as hell if I managed to convince you to leave just by seeing me," Ethan said.

Christian chuckled, giving the man a wink. "Sure, charming, we'll go with that."

"Okay, fine, I look good then."

Christian laughed, following Ethan to the bar as they ordered their drinks. It was the first time in a few months Christian had tried going out for drinks with someone. Then again, 'going out for drinks' on dating apps was generally just code for 'get a drink or two and go back to someone's house to get laid.' It was precisely the sort of setup he wanted when he'd found Ethan on the dating app the night before and struck up a conversation. After some brief wrangling, he'd secured a meetup and an agreement that if things went well, they'd go back to Ethan's place.

Normally, Christian was nervous during the first meeting, never knowing what to expect. Yet, as he chatted idly with Ethan and they waited for Christian's beer and Ethan's chocolate martini, he felt no trace of nerves. He honestly would have thought that meeting Ethan under false pretenses would have made his nerves worse than usual, but it had the opposite effect. Knowing the night would not end with him in Ethan's bed was a plus.

And that choice of a chocolate martini on the other man's part certainly made him feel better.

"So, you work at the base?" Ethan said as they moved back to the booth.

Christian nodded. "Yeah. Transferred in about a year ago, and it's looking like this will be my home for at least another year."

"At least? Sounds like you might not be sticking around," Ethan noted.

Christian shrugged. "I've been giving it some thought. I don't regret my time with the military, and it's given me a lot of good memories and skills. But I might take my life in another direction. I've got another year to decide, so there's no rush."

"So, what do you do?"

"Mostly administrative work, nothing exciting. I was never going to be in the thick of things, and while pencil pushing isn't the most exciting job, it is important," Christian said, sticking very close to the truth without giving it all away.

Ethan wrinkled his nose. "I'm sorry, but that sounds horrible."

Christian laughed. "Well, like I said, it isn't always fun, but hey, it pays the bills, and I don't have to worry about being thrown into a desert and getting shot at, so that's a plus."

"So, what, you going to take that and go somewhere with it if you get out? Do more work like that? Or hey, I bet it's given you a lot of experience with computers. You could do software or programming."

Christian shook his head. "Nah, my sister was the tech geek, not me. I'm thinking something in the mental health field. Maybe it'll just be administrative work there too, or maybe I'll buckle down and use that college pay we're supposed to be given, get a degree, and help people directly."

"Oh, that would be nice," Ethan said, his knee brushing Christian's as he took a drink.

Christian pressed his leg closer. "I'm not completely sure yet, but I'm toying with it. I think it could be good for me."

Ethan grinned. "And probably better money than you're making now."

"I hadn't thought of that, but yeah, you're right. The military doesn't start paying well until you get up a few ranks...and then some. And it would be nice not to be beholden to Uncle Sam the whole time I'm working," Christian admitted truthfully.

"That's always a plus."

Ethan looked down at his martini glass, shaking his head. "These things aren't very good. I'm pretty sure they didn't use cream, just a mix."

Christian laughed. "That your way of inviting me to drinks at your place instead?"

"Might just be," Ethan said, sliding his leg closer.

"Then I guess we should finish our drinks and head out," Christian offered.

Ethan winked, standing up. "Let me go to the bathroom real quick, and we can do just that."

Christian chuckled, watching the man as he paced toward the bathrooms. He waited until he saw him disappear around the corner before looking at Ethan's glass, which remained half-full. Knowing he didn't have much time, he reached into his pocket. Christian had debated with himself about how he would handle the situation and finally settled on making sure Ethan wouldn't be a problem once they got back to the apartment.

At first, he'd thought about sleeping pills, but then he realized he wouldn't know the correct dose, and he didn't know how much alcohol would be involved. The last thing he wanted was to seriously harm or kill the man, and he had nixed the idea. It was Lily who had given him the idea of how to get Ethan out of the way and provided him with a thumb drive's worth of helpful programs.

Taking the small baggy of crushed laxatives out of his pocket, he unwound the tie and dumped it into the drink. Using one of the stirring sticks provided in a holder, Christian mixed the finely ground pills in as quickly as possible. His heart raced furiously as he tried to get the powder to dissolve completely. He almost jumped out of his skin when he heard the fierce roar of the air dryer come to life in the bathroom. Trying to keep his breathing under control, he stirred furiously before finally giving it a quick stir in the other direction to stop the movement of the liquid and flinging himself back in his seat.

Ethan emerged a moment later, smiling as he approached

the table. Christian smiled back, dropping the stirring stick onto the floor with a silent apology to the staff who had to clean.

"Sorry about that. I've been drinking water non-stop today," Ethan explained as he sat back down.

"No worries. Not going to judge a man for staying hydrated," Christian said, waving him off.

Ethan raised his glass. "Well, cheers to a good night?"

Christian smiled, praying that everything was dissolved. "A very good one."

Ethan tipped his glass back, draining the contents. When he set the martini glass back down, all Christian could see was a bit of chocolate syrup at the bottom. Ethan, however, had wrinkled his nose in distaste.

"God, that is the worst mixture. Just gets more bitter near the bottom. Remind me to stick to normal cocktails and beer when I'm here," Ethan complained.

Christian chuckled, draining his beer. "Like you said, there are better drinks at your house, right?"

* * *

CHRISTIAN WASN'T sure what the normal rate for a cocktail server was, but whatever Ethan was making apparently went above and beyond Christian's pay rate. The leather furniture looked like it had been bought recently and not from a resale shop. The white carpet would have been expensive as hell to clean, but the apartment was lined with it as far as he could see and looked pristine. The tables and chairs all looked like they'd come out of a designer shop and had probably been made with the best wood. The display was a bit ostentatious for his tastes, but Christian had to admit it looked good.

However, the same couldn't be said for Ethan.

"Wow, nice place you have here," Christian mused as he looked around.

Ethan winced, a hand resting on his stomach. "Yeah, thanks. Cost me a bit, but it makes me happy."

"I bet it cost," Christian agreed.

Ethan gave a faint smile. "It's alright, I make pretty good money. And I've got something on the side that will also bring me a good load of cash. I'll be set."

Christian never realized how good his acting potential was until he flashed what felt like the most natural smile. "Yeah?"

Ethan nodded. "Oh yeah."

"Well, that must be nice. Not getting into trouble, are you?" Christian teased.

Ethan winced again, stepping toward the nearby hallway. "Nah, nothing like that. I'm a good boy."

Christian's lip curled, but he said, "Well, hopefully not too good."

Ethan chuckled, though the sound came out forced. "Not me, not ever."

Christian watched the other man, seeing indecision come over his face. Christian hadn't known how long it would take for the pills to kick in, but apparently, it had taken the time it took them to leave the bar and walk to Ethan's apartment complex. The man looked pained and a little green, and Christian bet he was trying to find the most covert and least embarrassing way to excuse himself.

"Something wrong?" Christian asked with concern in his voice.

Ethan shook his head. "No, no, I'm okay. But, uh, I think I need to go freshen up a little. You can make yourself comfortable and get a drink if you want. Everything's in the kitchen."

"Oh, sure, go ahead," Christian said, hoping he sounded politely confused.

Ethan chuckled again. "Don't worry, I'll just be down the hall if you need anything."

From the look on Ethan's face, however, Christian was betting the other man hoped he didn't need anything. Christian had never taken laxatives in his life, but he'd done a bit of research before he settled on using them. Apparently, taking one too many in a short time created an incredibly uncomfortable and messy result. Thankfully, though, Christian had noted it wasn't fatal.

"Okay, take your time. I'll...chill out here," Christian said, his eyes falling on the laptop on the coffee table and the flash drive beside it.

"Yeah, yeah. I'll be right back," Ethan said as he all but dashed down the hallway.

From the rather loud fart that echoed out of the bathroom as the door closed, followed by a distressed moan, Christian was betting the man wasn't quite as quick on his feet as he might have wished. If it weren't for the fact that he was privy to what Ethan was up to, Christian would have felt a genuine pang of guilt for what he'd done. As it was, he could push the nagging emotion out of the way and hurry over to the couch.

Thankful he didn't have to hunt for the computer and was far enough away from the bathroom, but where Christian's paranoid ears could hear if the door opened, he plopped down. Opening the lid, he waited until the screen lit up and displayed one profile to log into. Grimacing, he pulled out the small thumb drive in his pocket and tapped the spacebar to begin trying to log onto Ethan's computer. To his complete surprise, the login screen disappeared, showing a logo and then the home screen.

"Seriously, no password?" Christian muttered to himself.

Then again, he supposed he shouldn't be surprised. He knew far too many people in his age group and younger who weren't particularly careful about their security. That went double for people like Ethan, who lived alone. Since no roommate could snoop, he probably thought he was safe. Which was odd since he was not only comfortable with bringing relative strangers into his home but was also currently trying to blackmail someone he was paranoid would find a way to get to him.

"Alrighty then," Christian said with a shake of his head.

He'd been dreading the moment he'd have to get past a password screen. Having been spared that, he took the flash drive and pushed it into the computer's USB port. It took a moment, but the laptop pinged to signify it recognized it. He opened the folder containing the files and began digging through the drive.

It took only a minute, but he quickly found the folder he was looking for. To his even greater annoyance, the folder was labeled David. Rolling his eyes, he opened it, his brow rising as he found not only a video but a few dozen pictures as well. Almost before he could catch himself, Christian moved the cursor over one of the pictures, clicked, and then paused. Grimacing, he moved the cursor away and opened the video folder instead, remembering to hit the mute button at the last second as the video began to play.

His heart leaped as the familiar video started. Ethan had sent the first couple of minutes instead of any specific part. Having confirmed it was the right video, he looked at the timestamp, cocking his head as he realized the full length was over an hour.

"Damn, nice stamina, General," Christian muttered.

He transferred the full-length file to his thumb drive and promptly deleted all the pictures. For good measure, remembering the video had been edited, he found the folder for edited videos and deleted the copies there. After another moment's thought, he decided to check if Ethan was a liar as well as a blackmailer. Moving the cursor to the taskbar at the bottom, he smirked as he saw a cloud icon.

As he opened it, he jerked and heard the toilet flush. He sat there, waiting, his heart in his throat. The sound of the door never came as he sat there for what felt like an eternity. Heart still hammering, he returned to the screen and snorted as he found a copy of all the files in the online storage.

"An idiot, but not a complete idiot," Christian mused as he deleted them.

But also not bright enough to keep his things under lockdown. Christian chuckled, moving one of Lily's files on his thumb drive over to the hard drive and activating it. It was a small gift from Lily, who swore up and down that, given an hour or so, it would scrub everything in the background of Ethan's computer. If done right, it would make sure nothing deleted or indexed would be accessible, no matter how good the person was with computer systems. Content to let it run in the background, he put the laptop back on the table.

Pocketing the flash drive, he hummed contentedly. His good mood didn't stop when he heard the toilet flush again, followed by the sound of running water. Christian pulled his phone out, quickly opening a browser and idly scrolling as he heard the bathroom door open.

Ethan, still green in the face, leaned out from the hallway. "Hey, uh, I'm really sorry about this."

Christian peered up, eyes wide with concern. "Are you okay? You don't look so good."

"I think I ate something...wrong. Sorry, I know that's not what you wanted to hear," Ethan muttered, looking away.

Christian shook his head, pocketing his phone. "No, don't be sorry. It happens to the best of us. Do you need anything?"

"No, but I don't...I know, nothing will be happening

tonight, not with...this. Um, maybe another time?" Ethan offered, hopefully.

Christian smiled softly, nodding. "Don't worry about it. I'm sure you probably don't want company. You just worry about feeling better, alright?"

"Yeah, of course," Ethan said with another grimace.

Christian walked to the front door opening it. "Text me?"

Ethan put on a pained smile. "As soon as I'm better."

Christian nodded. "Looking forward to it."

The look of concern on his face melted as he closed the door behind him. Christian jogged down the stairs leading to the street and onto the sidewalk. As he pulled out his phone to order a ride back to the base, he also pulled out the thumb drive and stared at it with a wide grin.

"Definitely looking forward to it," he said.

DAVID

Sunday night found him staring at his ceiling rather than sleeping. It wasn't as if Christian had told him he would contact him regarding whatever he had planned, but David had hoped. He checked his phone repeatedly as he'd puttered around his home and kept it on his bedside table while it charged rather than in the living room.

With only a couple of hours sleep, David was forced to drag himself out of bed on Monday morning. The first thing he did was check his phone and found nothing. With a sigh, he showered and dressed. At least a dozen times, he considered trying to contact Christian, only to put it away and tell himself to wait.

The ride up in the elevator to the waiting room was the longest of his life, and David all but darted out when the doors opened. He paused as he spotted Christian behind his desk, already at work. The blond looked up, smiling before looking off to the side. It was then the general spotted someone else in the waiting room.

"Good morning, General," Christian called, his eyes settling on Reyes beside him.

"Good morning, gentlemen," David replied, nodding toward Reyes, who quickly stood to salute him.

Christian chuckled, patting Reyes' side. "Don't start doing that, or your arm is going to give out. He's in and out of his office all day and gets grumpy if he gets saluted every time."

"And he speaks from personal experience," David told him, still watching Christian.

Christian chuckled. "That I do. If you'd like to get started on your day, General, I'll be in with your coffee in a few minutes. You've got about an hour before any appointments, so don't feel rushed."

David nodded, hoping that was a good sign. David didn't normally take coffee in the morning, preferring water or tea. But if Christian was going to use that as an excuse for them to be alone, then David wasn't going to argue.

"That works, but spare the cream and sugar," David said, marching to his office.

He heard Christian talking softly to Oscar as David closed his office door behind him. Taking a deep breath, he purposefully made sure not to hurry, taking his time to sit down and organize his thoughts. When that didn't burn enough time before Christian came in, he powered up his computer and began to log in. As the computer brought up the confirmation screen, his door slid open.

Christian walked in with a huge, steaming mug. He closed the door, marched to the desk, and set it down with a heavy thud.

"Sorry about that. You looked like you hadn't slept all weekend, so I had to make it extra strong. Careful, I think it's more sludge than liquid," Christian said.

David took the mug by the handle, sniffed, and took a sip. "Oh. Yes, you're not kidding."

Christian smiled, reaching into his pockets. "And I'm sure you're wondering what I got up to over the weekend."

David grimaced at the extremely bitter coffee. "You could say that, yes."

"I'm honestly surprised you didn't get a phone call," Christian said.

"Why?"

Christian reached out, dropping something on the desk before pulling his hand back. David looked down, blinking at the small memory drive on the edge of his desk. Glancing up at Christian, David reached out to take the device.

"Is this…" David began.

Christian grinned. "The flash drive in question? That it is."

David pulled it closer. "You're sure?"

"If you're asking if I watched it, then no. I opened the only file, and it was the same two minutes I saw, but there was a total of sixty minutes on the video I found. I stopped once I realized what it was, though I have to say, I'm impressed by your stamina."

David chuckled as hope blossomed in his chest. "It was mostly foreplay."

"Ah, a man of taste as well as passion, I approve."

David grinned. "How did you manage this?"

"I told you I'd seen him on an app before. I messaged him when you and I were talking, and he responded quickly. He was also pretty quick to go on a date with me last night and took me back to his place."

David raised a brow. "You—"

"Did not sleep with him. A couple of laxatives in his drink was more than enough to end the night before we could get to the sexy parts he was hoping for. But since he was stuck in the bathroom, I might have entertained myself by digging around. And would you believe it? I found the thumb drive. I checked his computer for good measure, and he wasn't telling the truth about not saving it to the cloud. He also left out that he had a file on his computer, along with quite the picture collection."

David scowled. "Damn him."

"Oh, don't worry. I learned a few tricks from those friends of mine. Everything's gone, and he's not getting them back."

David held the drive up. "I can't believe you managed this."

"Hey!"

David shook his head, looking at Christian. "No, I just mean...I had no idea what you were planning, but I never expected this. You really...went on a date with him just to drug him with laxatives and steal this from him?"

Christian laughed. "I mean, normally, I'm not big on theft, but I figured I could make an exception for a guy who was blackmailing you. Thought it might even things out a bit."

"You won't hear any argument from me," David said.

Christian grinned. "Didn't think I would."

David closed his hand around the drive, making a tight fist. Maybe the entire thing would have been settled without Christian's interference. Certainly, David would have been out a big chunk of his savings, which he'd been spared because of the man standing before him looking proud of himself.

And maybe a little smug.

"Someone looks full of themselves," David noted.

"Maybe a little."

"It's well deserved, so perhaps you should be smug."

David had to admit he found the entire thing more than a little...arousing. He'd always known Christian was capable and thought above and beyond the box. Yet, this had required an entirely different set of skills, and while subterfuge shouldn't have been something David found admirable, it had been used for a good purpose. It had also required a great deal of thought, and Christian had been as thorough as he possibly could to make sure nothing was left.

David chuckled. "Well, I suppose that takes care of that, doesn't it?"

"It does."

David looked up. "Thank you."

Christian shook his head. "Don't. I'm just glad I was able to help."

"And take a peek into my private life," David added with a grin.

Christian ducked his head, laughing nervously. "I would like to stand here and say I didn't get a thrill from what I saw, but I won't start lying to you now. But I promise I didn't look at anything I hadn't already seen...even the pictures."

David smirked. "And considering how curious you are, just how tempting was it to take a peek?"

"On the grounds of not wanting to self-incriminate, I'm going to plead the fifth and restate that I looked at nothing in detail and deleted everything thoroughly," Christian said with pink cheeks.

It was, by far, the most flirtatious conversation David had ever had with Christian. It went well beyond what he usually allowed, even if it was tempting with someone as good-looking as Christian around. But considering his sudden good mood and the debt he now owed Christian, he found himself letting his strict standards slip a little. Well, and he'd never seen Christian blush so much since the man had laid eyes on David's naked body, and he found himself liking the attention.

"Well, I should probably...get back to my desk. Reyes is still looking at everything like he's never seen a computer or keyboard before, so I should make sure he's not having a stroke out there," Christian said, stepping back toward the office door.

David nodded, still holding tight to the drive. "Okay, we'll talk later."

Christian hesitated, looking like he wanted to ask for specifics. "Uh, okay."

David watched him go, his continuing lack of standards allowing him to stare at Christian's retreating ass as he left. After a moment, he returned his attention to the device in his hand, chiding himself for being foolish.

"Behave, old man," he reminded himself.

He was spared having to consider whether he was toeing a dangerous line by the sudden shrill ring of his phone. David jumped, forgetting he'd turned the ringer on and left it that way while waiting to see if he'd hear from Christian. Frowning, he pulled his phone out, smirking when he saw the unknown yet strangely familiar number.

David answered. "Ethan."

The man's voice came through in a high, angry shout. "How the fuck did you do it?"

David held the USB stick up again, eyeing it. "You're going to have to be more specific, Ethan. I do a lot of things throughout the course of my day."

"You know damn well what I mean! How did my stick disappear?"

David raised a brow, wondering how the solution hadn't already risen in Ethan's mind. Had David almost been done in by someone who did not top any intelligence charts?

David clicked his tongue. "You really should learn to keep a better watch over your things."

"Fuck you! I had it safe. You don't even know where I live! It's not even in my name. How did you know?" Ethan demanded.

"If you haven't managed to put the puzzle together by

yourself, then why do you expect me to put it together for you?"

"David, you absolute asshole!"

"I'll tell you what, I'll give you what you gave me. When you figure it out, go ahead and call me and let me know. But until that time, stand around and think real hard about your life choices. You almost had me this time, you try it again, and I'll bring you and anyone helping you down too."

"Don't threaten me, it would ruin you too!"

"Maybe. It depends on what you tried to throw at me. But the thing is, I would still have a career, even if it wasn't the same. But you? You'd end up in jail. And yeah, blackmail? That's a serious offense, especially when you're coming after a general, so you can count on getting a felony on your record. Keep that in mind the next time you decide you want to hold something over my head."

David ended the call before Ethan could think of anything else to add. Then, before Ethan could dial him back, David blocked the number. For good measure, he also went into his email and blocked the email address. Sure, Ethan could generate unlimited email addresses and probably spoof a phone number, but what would that matter? The man had nothing he could use to threaten David anymore; otherwise, he would have pulled it out on the phone call.

He was safe.

David set the flash drive on the desk, mentally tallying when he could leave the office to destroy the damned thing in peace. Once it was gone, everything would be perfectly safe again, and he could live peacefully. One day, he might even look back and laugh a little.

In the meantime, he had a new problem. The image of Christian rose in his mind, and David smiled. As much as their flirtation probably crossed a line or three, David was willing to push that aside for the moment. He owed Christian a great deal and needed to think of a perfect repayment.

An idea bubbled up in his mind, and his smile turned into a grin. And while it wouldn't cover the whole debt he owed Christian, it was at least a good start. David glanced at the clock on the computer, calculating when the end of the workday would come.

* * *

David stepped out of his office, stopping as he watched Oscar Reyes limp toward the elevator. The man looked like he'd slept better since the last time David had seen him, but his mood had darkened since that morning.

David looked at Christian. "Something go wrong?"

Christian shrugged. "He was like that after I came back from lunch."

David thought back, just as mystified as Christian. The only significant thing that happened was the monthly checkup visit from one of the clinic workers. Normally, David would go to the clinic, but since he sometimes forgot, Christian had taken it upon himself to bring one of them to David's office.

"Oh yeah, speaking of, how was Troy?" Christian asked.

David snorted at the thought of the chipper doc. "The same as usual, though quieter."

"Well, we chatty folk have our quiet days too."

"Today must have been his. When should I expect yours?"

Christian stuck his tongue out. "I reserve those for my days off."

"Ah, so a special occasion then."

"Yeah, it's not like I get much time off."

David inched closer to the desk to lean on it. With Christian watching him, he was suddenly more aware of what he was getting ready to say and felt a strange nervousness. Quietly, he reminded himself what he was offering was nothing unusual, especially considering what Christian had done for him.

"How's our schedule looking for the rest of the week?" David asked.

Christian hummed thoughtfully, turning his attention to his screen. "Not our worst week. I'd say we're doing pretty well. Though the Staff Sergeant was by again."

David winced. "From Maelstrom?"

"The very same."

He sighed. "I suppose I should have expected that. I've been getting reports that the team hasn't taken well to their newest member. Or rather, their newest member and the team leader aren't getting along. The rest are getting dragged along for the ride."

"That bad?"

"Yes, apparently, there was an issue during training. Well, a few, but one of them required a visit to the docs, who were not too pleased."

"Oh, that sounds nice."

"Yes, very nice."

It was a problem he'd foreseen, but it had once again prompted Philip to call him and warn, not so subtly, that he had been against the new addition to the team in the first place. David wasn't bothered, and he'd assured Philip everything was under control and he didn't need to worry. There were bound to be bumps in the road when bringing two different groups together, especially when strong personalities were involved.

David shrugged lightly. "I have something in mind for them anyway. I've just been letting them...get acquainted. Once the last of the paperwork has gone through, I'll give them something to focus on besides how much they don't like one another."

"Mm, another dastardly plan?"

"Something like that."

"I'm sure they'll love it."

David leaned forward. "So, I did have a reason for asking."

Christian looked up, blinking. "Oh, what's that?"

"Is there any point this week when things can be shuffled around so we can get out of here a little earlier than usual? Or better yet, a lot earlier?"

Christian cocked his head before turning his attention back to the computer. After a moment, he nodded. "Yeah, looks like Wednesday would be best. If I move things around a bit, Tuesday and Thursday will be a bit stuffed, but we could get out two hours early if we wanted. Why?"

David reminded himself silently that there was nothing wrong with what he was going to say.

David hummed. "Well, I've been thinking, considering what you did for me."

Christian interrupted. "I told you, don't worry about it."

"But I am worried about it, and you'll like it."

"Is that an order?"

David continued as though he hadn't been asked that. "It's going to be tricky to find a way to pay you back that won't get you all...puffy."

"I do not puff."

"But I think a good start would be treating you to what I hope is a good meal, with what I know are some good drinks."

Christian's prepared protest stopped short, and he looked quizzically at David. "Wait, dinner?"

David chuckled. "Yes. At my home, Wednesday night?"

"Are you cooking?"

"Believe it or not, I'm pretty good in the kitchen when I

want to be...and have the time. I can make you something delicious, and you can come over and enjoy yourself."

Christian stared at him for so long David began second-guessing himself. He'd been pretty sure it was a perfectly reasonable offer without sounding inappropriate or presumptuous. He didn't think it was either since, quite frankly, he didn't know if there was anything to presume. David quickly reminded himself that even if there was something to presume, nothing would happen.

Just a nice dinner.

Christian's face broke into a wide grin. "Alright, I can agree to that."

"Please, don't let me twist your arm," David said dryly.

Christian opened his mouth, then closed it with a snicker. "I'm not responding to that."

"Why?" David asked suspiciously.

"Because I'm not getting accused of sexual harassment in the workplace."

David couldn't help but widen his eyes, which made Christian laugh even harder.

"I'm kidding, c'mon. I would love to come over to your place and have dinner. But I'd rather do it because you want to, not because you feel obligated," Christian told him.

Was that the reason behind his initial hesitation? David couldn't help his scoff.

"I don't invite people home very often, and if I felt like I needed to give you something, it wouldn't be a visit to my home. Truly, I'm grateful for what you did, and I would like to do something nice in return, even if you'll only allow this one small thing."

Christian smiled in a way David thought was coy. "Okay. What time?"

"Would eight work for you? It'll give me time to get

home, start cooking, and have everything ready," David offered.

"Eight it is."

"Good." David smiled, delighted at how pleased Christian was.

It was only dinner.

CHRISTIAN

Nervously fiddling with his shirt, Christian rechecked the address. Looking up at the house, he squinted at the number printed on the side in bold numerals. All in all, it looked like he was in the right place, but somehow, he didn't equate the house with General Winter.

In the low light of the dying evening, Christian could see it was one-story and ranch-style. The house had a sizable porch, with a couple of chairs and a small table, looking out over the sea behind him. The lawn was well taken care of, full and green, and he couldn't make out a single weed. More surprising was the lush growth in a flowerbed running along the front of the house, against the half-wall that marked the property's perimeter and around the majestic weeping willow in the front lawn.

"Didn't even know those grew here," Christian commented as he eyed the tree.

There was a simple beauty to the design of the flower beds that Christian didn't see very often. It was obvious everything was well taken care of, probably with a dedicated and attentive hand. But instead of looking carefully laid out and meticulously planted, there was a sort of chaos, albeit controlled. Daisies mingled with lilies, and a few large flowering vines crept up trellises against the house's outer walls.

Grunting in approval, he stepped onto the front walk, which was also clear of weeds. The front steps looked well-used but safe, and as he looked over, he saw only one of the chairs had a cushion.

Looking at the front door, Christian cleared his throat and took a deep breath, forcing himself to knock. It felt oddly like showing up for a highly anticipated date, and he hadn't been able to shake the butterflies in his stomach from the moment he'd left work. Showering, shaving, brushing his teeth, and choosing his outfit had all been done with the care of someone going for a big night out. It didn't matter how much he told himself it was a friendly invitation. That meant absolutely nothing, and he couldn't relax.

The door swung wide, and General Winter stared at him through the screen door.

"Christian, you made it. And early, as usual."

"Ah, sorry, General, I wasn't thinking. Hopefully, I didn't put you off schedule?"

"I can promise you, I'm just as prone to being early as you are, so you're just in time. Come on in, and...call me David, please. This isn't supposed to be a formal occasion."

Christian nodded, taking the door as the general pushed it open for him. He had to remind himself to think of him as David. It's not like Christian didn't know General Winter's first name or anything, but he'd never called him by it, not even in conversation with another person. It seemed disrespectful to refer to the general he respected highly by his first name when his title and surname were far more appropriate.

He was led into a small entryway where he kicked off his

shoes and carefully aligned them with the boots and another ratty pair of shoes. There wasn't much of a hallway, only about four or so feet before it opened up into the rest of the house. More specifically, it opened into a spacious dining room with a solid table and eight chairs in the middle.

David chuckled, waving a hand toward the house. "I'm sure you're dying to look around, so go ahead."

"You know me too well," Christian said.

Christian wasn't about to pass up the opportunity, so he moved to the left of the table, where the space continued into a study with a small loveseat, bookshelves, and a desk with a computer. A set of closed double doors stood to his left, and Christian would hazard a guess they led to the master bedroom.

As he passed through the dining room, he spotted the kitchen to the right. The only thing separating it from the rest of the house was a wall where a fridge and stove sat and the large counter space, with three tall barstools facing toward the dining room. General Winter stood at the stove, bent over as he fussed with whatever was cooking.

To the right of the dining room, an arch opened up and dropped down into the living room. The furniture was dark leather, the large coffee table in front of the couch was glass-topped, and the legs looked like genuine wood. Against the far wall was a sizeable TV in an entertainment system lined with even more books than the study.

Going past the living room, another hallway, longer and wider than the others stretched back, and Christian saw two doors at the end, one on each side and another identical set halfway down.

General Winter's voice piped up from behind him. "That's only a couple of guest rooms, my workout room, and the second bathroom."

"Only?" Christian asked, thinking of his one-bedroom apartment with what was essentially a half bath.

"This was the house they gave me when I was first stationed here, so I've done what I can to try and make it a little more me," David explained.

Christian turned, deciding he probably didn't need to see the bedrooms. "I figured this was the one you chose."

David chuckled, disappearing back into the kitchen as he spoke. "Truth be told, this isn't far off what I'd have liked for my home if I'd had a choice. I could have had a choice, but this was the first place that opened up that they thought suited my position, and I took it. Been here for years, and I've been steadily working at it. The deck alone took me almost a year, and it's not even that big."

Christian rounded the corner, standing at the counter to watch David cook. He stood on the dining room side to stay out of the way.

"I didn't even see a deck," Christian admitted.

David nodded over Christian's shoulder. "I keep the windows on that side of the house shuttered at this time of night. There're so many windows in this house you'd be blinded at sundown."

Christian turned, realizing he was facing west, and nodded. Most of the west side of the house was large windows.

"Great during the morning and daytime, not so much in the evening," David continued.

"Is the backyard as nice as the front?" Christian asked.

"I certainly hope so, though Sara tells me no one notices the plants when I've got a jacuzzi on the deck."

Christian's eyes widened. "You have a hot tub?"

David chuckled. "I know it sounds a little hedonistic, but it serves a practical purpose. One of the things about getting older is, even if you keep yourself in decent shape, your body does start to protest. That thing has saved my back muscles more often than I could tell you."

"Doesn't hurt that it probably attracts people too," Christian teased.

David looked up after flipping something in the pan. "I told you, I rarely bring people here. If I'm going to…entertain, I prefer to do it in a hotel room."

Christian smiled. "Is it because you have a thing for younger guys? You don't want to be seen?"

"I wouldn't be telling the truth if I said that wasn't one of the reasons, and thank you so much for saying it with all the grace and subtlety I've come to expect from you," David said wryly.

"Hey, I'm not saying it to judge you," Christian told him.

And that wasn't just because Christian knew damn well if circumstances were different, he'd want to be one of those younger guys the general was into.

Christian drummed his fingers on the countertop. "Alright, what's the main reason you don't bring people here?"

"As much as I made it sound like this wasn't the home I chose, I have made it mine. Sara always said that even as a child, I was pretty territorial and preferred my own space. I suppose that's only gotten more intense as I've aged."

Christian plopped down on one of the benches. "You know, that's twice you've mentioned getting old, but you shouldn't."

David raised a brow, pulling the pan off the heat. "Oh? Closer to fifty than forty doesn't count as getting old?"

"I'm pretty sure you could still run paces around many of the soldiers on the base."

"Hmm, I should update the training schedule then."

"And you're not exactly carrying a lot of fat on you."

"A good diet and proper exercise will carry you for decades."

"And you've got the stamina to keep up with people younger than me."

"And there's the tact again."

"General."

"I told you to call me David."

"David."

"Yes?"

"You're a damn good-looking man who's in great shape. Stop talking like you're getting ready to keel over and die."

The slight smile forming on the general's face faded, and he looked up at Christian. Something in his pale green eyes made Christian's stomach tighten as he stared back. Christian didn't want to swear by it, but he couldn't help thinking there was something heated behind the cautiousness in the general's narrowing eyes.

"You know what they say about flattery, don't you?" General Winter asked.

"Reports are conflicting. At this point, I'm hoping the ones telling me it'll get me anywhere are accurate," Christian said with a cheeky grin.

"I suppose you'll have to find out."

"A little mystery in life never hurt anyone."

General Winter chuckled, pulling the pan from the heat and turning back toward the far corner, his back to Christian. It was the first time Christian remembered seeing the man in anything other than his uniform. Not that Christian could argue with his uniform; it was a good look for him. Yet seeing him in jeans and a loose button-up shirt was even more enticing than the video.

Well, in the immediate sense, anyway.

General Winter looked over his shoulder, smirking. "You've grown quiet."

"And you look like you're focusing."

He chuckled. "I hardly need to focus while I get the food onto plates."

Christian smiled. "Maybe I'm just thinking."

"That's a dangerous task, but it hasn't meant any danger for me so far."

"Maybe you just don't know what I'm thinking about."

"Or, maybe I do."

That stopped Christian short, and he gazed at General Winter with undisguised curiosity. If David sensed his stare, he was doing a damn fine job of pretending he didn't. It allowed Christian to watch him as he leaned over the plates, piling up what looked like greens, a few bits from the pan on top of beautifully seared fish. Watching him work steadily was oddly calming, even as he found his eyes constantly drifting to where the man's jeans hugged his ass just right.

"Do you think this is common?" Christian asked suddenly.

General Winter looked up, frowning. "Hm?"

Christian motioned between them. "I know people in our position are bound to be close, kind of just...part of the job, you know? As your assistant, I have access to you constantly, seeing you in all sorts of moods and whatnot, but...do you think everyone with a working relationship like ours also has...I don't know, uh—"

He trailed off, realizing what he was about to say. As comfortable as he felt, the sudden realization that the entire situation felt oddly intimate left Christian tongue-tied and with red cheeks.

General Winter chuckled. "Is it as personal?"

"Yeah," Christian said, now studiously admiring the countertop.

"No, I don't think so. Not that I possess statistics to say for sure, but I'd hazard a guess that few generals or bosses could depend on their assistants to have the sort of unwavering loyalty and desire to help you've shown. And I imagine even fewer can count on their assistants to become something like a friend to them over time without realizing it."

Christian looked up, unsure how to feel about such a platonic title. "Something like a friend."

General Winter turned around, holding two plates and a mysterious smile. "Something."

Christian followed him, again not sure what to say. There was clearly more going on between them than a casual dinner, yet neither was willing to say it aloud. If it was clearly one situation over the other, Christian would know exactly how to act or at least have a better idea. As it was, he wasn't sure if he should be treating him as General Winter, his superior and a man due a great deal of respect and deference, or as David, a good-looking man whose green eyes sent a pang of longing through him whenever David looked at him.

"Would you prefer to eat here or on the back deck?" General Winter asked him.

"Didn't you say the sun was blinding at this time of day?"

"I did, but it's later now."

Christian smiled. "Then lead the way."

DINNER PROVED to be better than he'd expected. Christian was no expert, but he knew good fish when he tasted it and when it was cooked properly. The fish had been rich, cut through with citrus and just a hint of spice to catch the back of the throat. The greens had been refreshing, with a slight zing of some vinaigrette. The wine David had pulled out of the cellar had been fantastic and complimented the dish perfectly with its rich, fruity flavors and complex sweetness.

And to go with the meal had been a magnificent sunset. By the time they'd come outside, the brightest colors had faded, allowing them to see perfectly. As they ate their meal, Christian savoring every bite, the bright orange and vibrant red had given way to deep purple and the faintest trace of a mellow blue. One by one, the stars peeked out, reflecting off the ocean a few dozen yards away, and the fireflies had come out in full force.

All perfect, and all before he could even address the company.

David chuckled. "So, you managed to sneak all those boys into the basement, and your foster parents never realized?"

Christian shrugged. "They were, uh, not the most attentive people. Okay, fine, Alice, the mom, had to take sleeping meds to get through the night, and her husband, uh, Andrew, was a bit of a drinker. If you didn't make an entire herd of elephants go through the house, you could pretty much do whatever you wanted after eleven at night. So yeah, the other two foster kids and I dragged some guys back to the house."

"I can only imagine what sort of trouble you got up to unsupervised," David said with a twinkle in his eyes.

Christian held a hand to his chest in mock affront. "Me? I was a perfect angel. I enjoyed long, philosophical conversations with them, discussing current events. No misbehaving or excessive making out ever happened."

David smirked. "I know things change with every generation, but I have a feeling teenage late-night parties haven't changed that much."

"Probably not," Christian said with a laugh.

David eyed his glass. "More wine?"

Christian eyed his already empty glass and gave it some

thought. "I don't know if I should, or I'll have to be wheeled out of here."

"Goes right to your head, eh?"

"Something like that."

"A good thing I have guest rooms then."

Christian hesitated. "Are you inviting me to stay the night?"

David cocked his head slowly. "I'm saying you are welcome to."

Was that the same as being invited, or just a simple courtesy? Christian knew which one he wanted it to be, and he knew damn well he did want more wine. The two of them were finally getting to where they didn't have to skip and swerve around every conversation, feeling as if they had to keep it going in one specific direction. Maybe it was the wine, but if that were the case, Christian would happily accept more.

"Pretty sure we polished off the bottle already," Christian pointed out.

"And I'm sure I have a few more bottles like it. I rarely dive into my wine supply. Having good company over to indulge sounds like a wonderful excuse," he said.

Christian watched General Winter for a moment, who was quickly becoming David in his mind. The older man was watching him in return, a wary hope in his eyes as the alcohol worked to bring down the layer of emotional barriers he kept up through his everyday life. David had undone the top button of his shirt, and Christian could see the sparse hair he knew peppered his chest. It reminded him of what he'd accidentally seen in that video, and he felt his gut tighten.

There was no way to be sure, but Christian knew accepting the general's offer was to accept another invitation. The one they'd been working their way up to for who knew how long, and Christian wasn't even sure he could trace how long, even if he tried. They had both been playing with fire from the moment they agreed to be alone in a casual environment, with no chance of anyone coming across them. Now was the moment where Christian had to choose, just as David did by offering, if he would stay or go.

Christian smiled. "No need to let a good opportunity pass, right?"

DAVID

The second bottle had been a good choice, in his opinion. Much like second bottles went, it tasted so much better than the first. If the eager way Christian was drinking was any indication, David wasn't the only one enjoying himself. He'd never realized how much he would enjoy the sight of Christian sitting on his patio, legs resting on the table, bare feet sticking up in the air as they talked. The man looked completely at home, and David hoped they could do this more often.

Even better, they'd positioned their chairs together, facing the sea. As they talked, Christian's arms and hands grew more animated as they emptied more glasses of wine. He'd pulled his shirt sleeves up, exposing the light blond hair on his toned arms. It meant that whenever Christian gestured wildly, his arms bumped against David, momentarily passing their warmth to him as Christian talked.

Christian hummed as he thought. "Did your dad get to see you become a general?"

David nodded. "I was a general for a few years before he passed. Told me that seeing his son do better than he did was something every father wanted. One of the only times I ever saw him with tears in his eyes."

"Aw, that's sweet."

David shrugged. "I suppose that's one way of putting it. I honestly just stood there in complete shock when it happened. I barely managed to return the salute he gave me and almost broke into tears myself when I finally did."

It felt strange talking about his parents when Christian's only measure of family was the two sisters he'd met in foster care. If it bothered Christian, it didn't show. On the contrary, David couldn't help but notice happiness on his handsome face. There was a wide, warm smile as he shared in David's story. David wanted to blame the alcohol for the urge to cross the distance between them and kiss the man stupid, but he knew the drinks were only making what he'd wanted in the first place even stronger.

"My parents were good people, and they loved me a lot. They had been trying for years, but two years before they had me, my mom was told she was never going to have kids. Then boom, a year and a half later, I came along. I guess I was spoiled, being a bit of a miracle child and all," Christian said with a light laugh.

"I think most people would be a little indulgent."

"Probably, maybe, I don't know. But I wasn't spoiled rotten; I was taught to say please and thank you, learned my manners, and did not act like a total brat. My mom was into reading and always tried to get me to read books. She started by reading to me when I went to bed. I think she wanted me to want to read them myself eventually, but I just loved the way she read. She always did these little voices, and sometimes brought my dad in to act stuff out. I think she was an actress in another life or something. But hey, why would I want to read them myself when my mom was better at it than I would ever be?"

David watched a wistfulness pass over Christian's face as he talked about his parents. His tone had a definite note of sadness, but his eyes glimmered with remembered happiness. David's parents had lived full lives, and as far as he knew, neither of them had gone with regrets. If anything, they had looked upon their lives, happy they had succeeded and were loving and loved in return.

David smiled. "I'm sure they'd be proud as hell to see what sort of person you've become."

Christian looked at him, eyes watery. "You think? I wonder sometimes."

"Why?"

"Truth be told, I'm not even sure I'm doing something I want. It's not that I don't enjoy working for you because I've grown to love it. But to continue serving in the military, should I renew my contract next year? I'm not so sure."

"Makes sense, considering you said you joined to ensure you had a roof over your head and food on the table."

"Not the most honorable reason."

"Maybe your reasons weren't noteworthy, but that doesn't mean you're not...honorable. You've got a spotless record, with plenty of commendations, and if I could, I'd give you more for what you did for me recently. I'd say it's more honorable to come into the service without noble intentions, follow through on your duty, and go above and beyond what was expected of you. I think that's someone worth being proud of, especially if it was your child."

That earned him a smile, and Christian turned his face away. "It's a nice thought."

David turned his attention away from Christian, allowing the man to collect himself at his own pace. The moon had risen, creating a wide beam of light reflecting off the calm water. It wasn't calm enough to reflect the dim light of the stars, but David contented himself, as he had so many times before, in watching the gentle scene. It was the first thing that sold him on staying in the house when he'd first been assigned to the base, and he'd never stopped loving it, even after a decade.

Christian cleared his throat. "This has been really nice. Honestly, I didn't know what to expect when I showed up. I know we talked about how casual the whole thing has been, but I never realized how much I needed it. I've never been very good at the going out and having a good time at bars or clubs thing. But this? Sitting with someone special, having good food, drinks, and great conversation? That's the sort of thing I live for."

"Someone special, eh?" David asked.

Christian didn't flush or look away this time. Instead, he held David's gaze. "Yeah."

David hadn't been so blind as to miss the attraction they shared. He suspected they had been eyeing each other longer than they would admit. David's offer for Christian to stay the night had been innocently phrased, but deep down, it wasn't all he was asking. Sex was on the table and probably had been from the moment he'd invited Christian to his home. He was sure he could integrate it into what he and Christian were. Sex was just sex.

But that one little phrase regarding Christian was different, equally terrifying, and wonderful in its insinuation. Yet, the fact that nothing happened meant there was still a chance one of them could back away without any worry about what would happen. All it would take was for them to go their separate ways, step back from the situation, and never acknowledge it again.

Christian's eyes darted over David's face. "So—"

David raised a brow. "Yes?"

"I have a question."

"I figured as much."

"And if it's too invasive, just tell me."

David snorted softly, looking down at his hands. Anticipation sent his heart racing as he wondered if Christian was finally treading the ground they'd been dancing around.

David looked up. "The video?"

"Yeah."

"What about it?"

"Are you...like, do you usually prefer younger guys?"

"I've never dated a younger man before, or at least not one that age. I find most of them physically attractive. But truth be told, they rarely have the emotional maturity I'd need in a romantic partner."

"I guess that makes sense."

David looked him over. "Why do you ask?"

"Would I get away with saying I was just curious?"

David laughed. "Probably not, no."

"Would I get away with saying I've been thinking about what I saw in that video a lot since then and still be able to blame it on the alcohol?"

"I suppose that depends."

Christian cocked his head. "On?"

"On whether or not you wanted me to take it seriously."

"I've been thinking about it a lot. And that's not just the alcohol talking. Well, a little, but not like...all of it."

"Just enough to give you courage?" David asked.

"And maybe the right level of stupidity."

David turned toward him, even more aware of how close they were. Christian had slowly angled himself, so his upper body faced David. Reading body language was a skill David firmly believed came with the territory of being a general or being in command. It was important to know when a subordinate was going to be trouble, when they would be willing, and when they were calm or irritated. It didn't require his extensive experience to understand that Christian's gradually opening arms, spread legs, and turned torso were an invitation.

"I kind of like the theory that it's more courage than stupidity," David told him.

"I guess we'll see," Christian said, turning his bright blue eyes on him.

Where he might have been debating with himself only moments before about whether to follow through, David found his answer as he gazed at Christian. Without hesitation, he reached out, taking hold of Christian's jaw and cupping it gently. As he pulled the man closer, a small smile curled at the corner of his lips, and he heard Christian's breath catch just moments before their lips met.

The hesitation didn't last long, though, and David felt Christian suddenly come alive as the kiss extended for more than a few seconds. Warm hands pushed into David's hair as Christian pulled him even closer. Chuckling, David parted their lips, letting his tongue dance over Christian's and drawing a low, needy moan from the younger man.

David stroked a hand down Christian's arm, gripping to feel the toned muscles under his skin and the warmth against his cool fingers. Before he could do much more, he felt Christian rise from his seat. A moment later, Christian was easing forward, sliding onto David's lap eagerly. Warmth and pressure landed on David's crotch as Christian made himself comfortable, hunching forward to continue their kiss.

David wasn't going to argue with the position, as it gave him ample opportunity to run his hands over Christian's shoulders, down his back, and finally to cup his ass. Growling appreciatively, David squeezed it, relishing the slight groan from Christian.

Feeling more than a little greedy, David gripped the bottom of Christian's shirt and yanked it over his head. Christian broke the kiss, shimmying out of the shirt before pressing their lips together again. David ran his hands up and down Christian's sides, gripping his hips and stroking the warm skin. Muscles rippled and danced beneath taut skin, following each of David's light touches.

"No offense, but if this is going to continue, I'd prefer somewhere where there's more room to get comfortable," Christian told him.

"I think my bed will serve just fine for that," David told him.

Christian quickly scrambled off his lap to let him up, drawing a low chuckle from David. Despite being older, he appreciated the vitality and energy younger men approached sex with. For all his maturity and emotional stability, Christian was no different than his peers in that regard. He marched into the house in front of David, shirtless and utterly unaware of the gorgeous sight he made.

David stepped ahead of Christian, wrapping an arm around his waist and pushing him against the wall with a hearty shove. Christian gasped, but his back arched, and he greedily held onto David as the distance closed between them again. David's hands once more roamed Christian's body, soaking up every piece of skin he could find. He took a moment to undo the button and zipper to the man's jeans, giving them a shove as he held Christian against the wall.

"You're going to have me naked before we hit the bedroom," Christian whispered with a chuckle.

"That's the idea."

Christian shimmied out of his jeans, kicking them to the side. David's eyes roamed further south, raising a brow as he realized there was no underwear to remove. Instead, Christian's hard, straining cock jutted up between them, inviting David's hands to wrap around it and stroke a thumb teasingly over the already leaking head.

"I see," David said in approval as he teased Christian's cock.

Christian whimpered, back arching further into his touch. "David—"

That soft sound of desperate need shot straight to David's groin, making his pants even tighter. He'd been with enthusiastic partners and some who were downright demanding. David didn't think he'd ever heard someone who knew him like Christian speak with such utter desire, to the point that Christian's voice was weak and breathless. It was intoxicating, and David found himself stroking Christian with more fervor, drawing ever more plaintive sounds from him.

However, Christian was not one to stand by idly and be teased, and with a bit of wriggling, he managed to get his hands between them. David sucked in a breath as he felt the pressure against his cock ease while Christian worked the buttons. A moment later, a deep noise rumbled up from his throat as Christian's hand shoved into his underwear, wrapping his warm fingers around the girth of David's cock.

"Oh fuck," Christian moaned, pulling it free.

"Didn't see that in the video," David pointed out.

"Glad I didn't. Would have ruined the surprise."

Christian's eagerness stoked the already roaring flames inside David. Whether because of his building lust, the wine, or some combination, he could feel his head spinning as he took Christian's lips once more. He could taste the mixture of wine and Christian on the man's tongue, jutting his hips forward to stroke his cock alongside the man's grip.

"I need you...to fuck me," Christian said against his lips.

"Eager," David noted.

"Foreplay another time, your cock in me now," Christian shot back.

David grinned. "Then maybe you should get to my bed, face down, with that ass pointed toward me."

He stepped away from Christian as he said it, and to both his amusement and arousal, Christian was quick to comply. The man's eyes lingered a moment longer on David's thick cock before heading toward the double doors that led to David's bedroom. David pulled at his shirt, hearing the double doors open, and once he could see again, he followed.

By the time he was stripped of his clothing, he'd entered the bedroom. Against the back wall lay his unnecessarily large but incredibly comfortable bed. It was a sight for sore eyes at the end of a long, hard day. But it looked even better with Christian lying on his stomach, looking back over his shoulder in expectation.

David strode forward, running a hand from Christian's ankle over his calf to his thighs. He ran his fingers through the thicker hair, smiling when the younger man jumped as David's touch slid along the sensitive skin on the man's inner thighs. His eyes darted from the delicious curve of his plump ass along the pale skin of his back, the faint freckles on his shoulders, and the blue eyes that never left David's face.

"I'd apologize for being impatient," David said as he approached the bedside table. "But I suspect you're not feeling much different."

Christian pushed himself up. "How are you so calm right now?"

David pointed at him, then at the bed. "Remain lying down."

Christian's eyes widened, first with surprise, but David didn't miss the sudden light of arousal in the man's expression as he laid back down. His words hadn't been harsh, but General David Winter knew how to command without barking or raising his voice. Satisfied Christian was behaving himself, David retrieved a condom and bottle of lube from the drawer.

David walked around the bed and knelt at the end so he

was positioned behind Christian. As he opened the condom wrapper, he took the time to admire the sight. If he watched closely, he could see a slight tremble in Christian's shoulders as he waited.

"How long have you been wanting this?" David asked as he rolled the condom on.

Christian let out a shaky laugh. "Longer than I thought, apparently."

"Never thought you'd be here, lying on my bed, presenting yourself so your general would fuck you, eh?"

Christian let out another soft noise. "No."

"No?"

"Shit. No, *sir*."

David smirked, watching Christian tense again and spit out the correction. It was a game David tried here and there, and he was pleased to find Christian playing along, and happily at that. Grinning, he scooted forward, laying a hand on Christian's lower back.

"Hips up," he told him.

Christian pushed himself back, raising his ass in the air but staying face down on the bed. It was amusing and incredibly erotic to see the playful, teasing side of Christian disappear in the face of being commanded by David. Still taking in the sight laid out before him, David smeared a heavy layer of lube over his cock. With that done, he placed the blunt head of his cock at the entrance to Christian's ass.

That was enough to draw another low noise from Christian. David quickly found he loved the sounds Christian made, and he wondered what other sorts of noises he could draw from the man before the night was over.

CHRISTIAN

Fuck, he didn't think his heart had ever beat so hard and so fast. As he lay there, feeling the thick tip of David's cock teasingly pressing into him, Christian felt as though time had stalled. His whole body was taut as a wire, brimming with need.

One minute, they'd been talking, dancing carefully around the accidental touches, the alcohol making them comfortable, and the thoughts running wild in the back of their minds. Then, the next, Christian had found the courage to finally leap into the fray, needing to know if his thoughts and desires were his alone.

The touch had been incredible, and the kiss had seen his hopes realized. Everything that followed, however, had been beyond anything Christian dreamt. David had become something else entirely, someone else entirely. He was still remarkably calm, though Christian had felt the tremble in the man's fingertips and heard the deep roughness of desire in his voice when he spoke. But he spoke calmly, even as he pinned Christian against a wall. Or even, when he commanded him, keeping Christian on a leash with only his words.

And now he was pushing inside him.

Christian's breath caught in his throat as he felt the blunt head nudge into him. He forced himself to exhale slowly as David inched forward, spreading Christian even further. To the older man's credit, he paused, letting Christian adjust to the sudden intrusion before moving in another couple of inches, only to wait again.

Christian's head spun as David filled him completely, his hips against Christian's ass. Pressing his forehead against the softness of the bed, Christian took another deep breath. His ass burned, but he welcomed the not-so-dull ache as he felt the throb of David's cock. Behind him, David's hand lay comfortably against his lower back, stroking in slow, leisurely lines as he waited patiently.

"You okay?" David asked, hips still.

Christian nodded, feeling his body release its tension. "Yeah, yeah, I'm good."

David bent forward, laying a gentle kiss between Christian's shoulder blades. His warm breath gusted across Christian's skin.

"You feel amazing."

Christian couldn't think what to say but was spared having to think too hard when David decided to move his hips. It was slow at first, easing back before moving just as carefully forward. Christian felt a low moan draw deep from the depths of his throat as David's cock filled him again. The burn of David's cock gave way to a growing thrum of pleasure, curling his fingers against the bedspread beneath him.

David's hips jerked, driving in the last half with a sharp snap of his hips. The thick head of the man's cock brushed something inside him, drawing a cry from Christian as his nerves came to life.

That was all David needed apparently, and moving his hands to grip Christian's hips, he began to thrust in earnest. Skin met skin, the sound mingling with the cries rolling from Christian's throat. David's fingers gripped his waist, pulling him back into his thrusts with strong, calloused hands.

Sweat ran down his back as David's cock battered him from the inside. The thrusts pushing him into the bed, pinning him in place. Held as he was, Christian could do nothing but stay still, crying out as David repeatedly struck the bundle of nerves inside him, dragging wave after wave of pleasure through him with expert movements.

Before he realized what was happening, he felt himself being moved. A low gasp escaped him as he felt David pull out, and his body lifted upward. Then, he was on his back, his hips nudged to lay upon David's thighs.

Christian looked up, panting and needy but not blind to what knelt before him. David's toned chest was covered in sweat, hair glistening in the light from the bedroom door. His eyes were locked on Christian's face, pale and almost completely darkened by his swollen pupils, filled with lust. David's chest rose and fell rapidly as he reached down, realigning himself before pushing into Christian again.

Wrapping his legs around David as quickly as he could, Christian arched his back, lifting his body off the bed and pushing into the thrusts. His cock throbbed and ached with a need for release, but he found himself begging for David's cock. Heat and pleasure washed through him in alternating waves as David thrust again.

Christian didn't have long to enjoy the ride before David's hand wrapped around his cock, jerking it slowly. A strangled noise tore from Christian's throat as his strength gave out, falling to impale himself on the next inward thrust. It took only a few strokes of his painfully hard cock before

Christian gave another cry, his fingers digging into David's thighs as he came.

Even as the pleasure crashed through him, Christian felt David throb deep inside him. The older man bowed over, pressing his face into Christian's chest as his body jerked. Christian felt himself spatter them both as his cock twitched between them, his body singing with thought-erasing pleasure.

Christian slumped, helpless to continue holding himself up as his orgasm finally left him. Above him, David pulled out carefully, his arms shaking as he slowly pushed himself back and eased Christian's legs onto the mattress. Christian watched, unable to find the strength to move as the older man paced around the bed toward a darkened doorway nearby. There came the sound of rustling and then running water before David returned.

David smiled crookedly, sitting on the bed beside him and bringing a damp cloth up to wipe Christian's body clean. They said nothing as the warm rag was gently wiped up and down Christian's torso, his hips, and around his groin. Christian reached out, slowly stroking David's thighs as he allowed himself to be cleaned.

Still saying nothing, David stood up, returning the cloth to the bathroom. When he returned, he carefully pulled the covers over Christian.

"Not coming?" Christian asked, worry ruining his cozy lethargy.

David chuckled. "I need to lock up and turn the lights off. Stay here and get comfortable."

"Is that an order?" Christian asked with a weak chuckle.

David bent forward, smirking. "I see your sense of humor has returned."

"It left?"

"When you wanted me to fuck you into the mattress, it did."

Christian grunted, his mind enjoying the sound, but his body was far too tired and tender for anything more. Instead, he leaned forward, kissing the other man.

"And if you're good, you can do it again before we go in tomorrow morning."

David returned the kiss, lingering for a moment longer. "Promises, promises."

"Why do I get the feeling work just got a lot more interesting?" Christian asked.

David's smile flickered. "We'll see. I'll be right back."

It wasn't the most comforting of responses, but Christian didn't have the energy to fight. He knew they had crossed a serious line by sleeping with one another just once. To go further would invite even more potential for disaster, and that on the heels of David having already been threatened with the same danger from someone else.

But Christian knew a good piece of advice when he heard one, and he allowed himself to curl up against the pillow as David went to tend to the rest of the house. It allowed him the perfect view of David's naked body as the general padded through the house, turning off lights and, from the sounds of it, cleaning up a little.

Christian closed his eyes, thinking he might just get used to this.

CHRISTIAN HAD SPENT most of his day humming as he worked. As far as Thursdays went, it was one of his better ones, and he was enjoying himself thoroughly. Sure, maybe he hadn't got quite as much sleep as he was used to, and his ass was more tender than usual, but Christian wasn't going to complain about either.

It didn't hurt that he had a night of great memories to run through his head as he slogged through reports, fielded calls, and dealt with irritated soldiers all day. Even better, he saw a reminder of his good memories walking in and out of his office while the general dealt with his daily tasks.

Reyes glanced at him, frowning for the twentieth time in an hour. "You good?"

Christian looked up from his screen. "Yeah, why, should I not be?"

"You've been singing all day. Not sure if I should be worried you're on drugs or drunk."

Christian laughed. "You might be happy to be grumpy all day, but that doesn't mean the rest of us have to be."

"I'm not grumpy," Reyes protested.

Christian thought about it. "Hmm, you know, you haven't been as grumpy the past few days. Something good happen?"

"I'm not sure I like the idea of my being less grumpy suddenly."

Christian grinned. "Oh? So, something did happen. Are you just enjoying the sunny warmth of my company, or is it something else?"

"You can go back to singing now."

Christian held up a finger. "Oh, I know! You found yourself a date for the Gala!"

Oscar scowled. "What?"

Christian rolled his eyes. "The big gala that's held like...every year. Pretty much every soldier shows up, if they can, all dressed up with their dates. Big names from the town are invited. It's a nice touch, bringing people in so they can see the better side of the base rather than just a few rowdy, drunken soldiers occasionally."

"Fancy parties aren't really my thing."

"Hmph, shame. I think you'd look good in your dress blues."

For a moment, he thought Reyes would say something in return, but instead, the man just turned back to his work. Oscar Reyes was a strange man, and his moods didn't always make much sense to Christian. Yet, there was something different about him, and had been for a couple of days. Christian wasn't sure what the other man was going through, but whatever it was, it had obviously been taking its toll. Christian hoped, for Reyes' sake, that his recent upturn in mood meant something good had finally happened.

The office door opened, and General Winter popped his head out to look around the room. Nothing had been different between them throughout the day, which Christian considered a blessing. He still wasn't sure what the hell they were. Whether the night before had been significant beyond a one-night thing, he knew it was important that nothing on the surface changed.

That didn't mean his heart didn't skip a beat or two when he saw the older man's handsome features.

"Need something?" Christian asked.

"Checking to see if we had any impromptu visitors to worry about at the moment," General Winter said with another glance around.

Christian shook his head. "No, sir. I closed the office about an hour ago so we wouldn't have to worry about it."

"And why, might I ask, did you do that?"

Christian laughed. "No offense, General, but you have a few things on your plate. If it's an emergency, they can call ahead like any reasonable person."

General Winter sighed. "That's fair. Speaking of which, since we have no one to worry about now, would you come in here?"

Christian nodded, looking at Reyes. "You okay to handle the phones?"

"I think I can manage."

Christian chuckled as he stood. "Glad to hear."

Grabbing his tablet, Christian followed the general into his office. As much as they both trusted his memory when it came to anything they discussed, Christian didn't like to take chances. He always brought his tablet to ensure he could take notes in case he forgot anything later.

Christian closed the door behind them. "Any word on our wayward team?"

General Winter sighed as he sat behind the desk, motioning toward the seats across from him. "Maelstrom hasn't arrived at the rendezvous point as quickly as I hoped. The Canadian wilderness isn't exactly known for being kind, but I hoped they would have more luck than this."

Christian frowned. "You don't think anything's happened to them, do you?"

"I hope not, but I won't dismiss the possibility. If they haven't arrived by the designated date, we'll send a rescue team to retrieve them. I won't lose faith in them, though. Team Maelstrom is good, and their intel officer, for all his recent infamy, is good too."

"Well, I hope it gets them to work together."

General Winter snorted, leaning back in his seat. "Well, then maybe it might not be too bad if something has happened. There's nothing quite like a block in the road to make or break a team."

"Which I suppose is better than staying stuck in this feuding limbo forever," Christian noted.

General Winter inclined his head. "Indeed."

Christian watched the other man, waiting for him to reach the next point, but he was distracted. Christian had never noticed before, but there was something alluring about watching the general as he worked. The man had always cut a handsome figure, but sitting in his chair, back straight, looking thoughtful but confident, only enhanced his good looks.

Christian was beginning to realize he might have a kink for men with authority.

David raised a brow. "Something wrong?"

Christian shook his head, looking down at his tablet. "No, sir, I'm okay."

There was a pause, followed by the general clearing his throat. "Okay, well, the door is closed, and there are no recording devices here, so why don't you share what's on your mind?"

Christian chuckled nervously. "I was just distracted for a moment...by you."

"By me."

Christian winced. "I apologize. I guess being alone with you has me letting my guard down for a moment. I also blame you for being so damned good-looking."

The corner of David's mouth twitched. "Is that so? Then maybe we should talk about how distracting it is to walk out of my office and find you bent over."

Christian blinked. "What? Hey! I knocked my mouse off the desk and was getting it back."

"That changes nothing from my point of view."

Christian ducked his head again, if only to hide the faint color that came to his cheeks. While it was a little odd to be so freely and openly flirting, it was a relief. It meant they weren't pretending there wasn't tension born of their sexual chemistry from the night before.

But it still didn't answer his other question.

Christian squirmed in his seat. "I don't...want to presume anything, sir, but...I do have a question."

"From the sounds of it, you're about to ask something that doesn't require a 'sir' placed in front of it," David said.

"Oh...right. Look, last night was great. I mean, hell, it was amazing. You're a good-looking man and an amazing lover, and as a man, you're someone I respect deeply and care about."

David blinked slowly, a ghost of a smile on his face. "I would return the favor, but you've beaten me to every compliment."

Christian grinned. "Gotta be faster."

However, he could tell David was waiting, and Christian barreled on.

"The point is, I could...see myself enjoying something a little more...long-term."

"I see," David said slowly.

"And I know...what you said last night about not wanting something long-term with someone young," Christian continued.

David held up a hand. "Before you continue, I can see where this is heading, but I have to stop you there. If I were to choose not to enter into anything long-term with you, it wouldn't be due to a lack of maturity on your part. I'd like to say I've known you long enough to state with great confidence that you possess a deep well of maturity, intelligence, and a good heart that would make you a very attractive long-term partner."

Christian smiled at the compliment, but he didn't miss the catch. "I'm sensing a 'but' somewhere in there."

David's smile turned pained. "But our situation is not that simple, is it?"

No, it wasn't. David might be able to avoid a scandal if he were dating a younger man in a perfectly reasonable, sellable relationship. But there was no getting around the fact that a relationship between a superior and subordinate, especially when it involved a general, was blatant fraternization. The night before had been enough to get them both into trouble. To enter into something more would just increase the risk.

"I understand, sir," Christian said softly, heart sinking.

"I'm not saying 'no.' I'm saying this situation requires...some thought. You're an amazing person, Christian, and I would hate to see your life ruined, as well as my own because we didn't think things through. Last night was wonderful, but if we're going to risk so much, we need to be sure it's worth that risk," David told him with a grimace stretching his features.

"Well, for what it's worth, for me, it's worth it," Christian said.

David opened his mouth, closed it, then opened it again. "I'll be honest. I'm not quite sure yet."

Christian nodded, his attention back on his tablet. "Like you said, not 'no' but—"

"Not what you wanted to hear," David admitted, voice soft.

It wasn't, not in the slightest, but Christian wouldn't lose his mind over it. It tugged at his heart, weighing it down for the first time all day. Still, he could take comfort in not being outright denied.

Christian cleared his throat. "So, I imagine you want to discuss the finer details of the Gala on Saturday."

David's pale eyes searched his face before nodding. As Christian watched, the strained, almost pained expression on the general's face faded, replaced by professional focus.

"Those from Command who accepted my invitation will arrive tomorrow at approximately 1300. We'll need to make sure their temporary housing is up to par. We also need to ensure the catering company has confirmed the appointment," General Winter began, looking over at his screen.

Christian nodded. "I've spoken with the company, but I'll

speak to them tomorrow evening to make sure everything is on track."

"Good, I don't want an incident like last year's."

"Not on my watch, sir."

"Good. Now, a few other things have been brought to my attention. Let me pull them up."

Christian nodded, waiting for the other man as he began to search for what he needed. It was easier to focus on the task at hand now they had settled the elephant in the room. The weight of the elephant had shifted to his heart, but at least he could focus.

So, that was something, at least.

DAVID

He could say with a hundred percent certainty that the annual Gala was not his favorite part of the year. It signaled the arrival and the culmination of the one aspect of his job he did not enjoy, politicking. David supposed it wasn't strictly politicking, it was more showing off and saying all the right things. More presentation and pomp than wheeling and dealing, but he considered it the same thing when it boiled down to it.

He looked over the hall full of decorations, soldiers, and guests, all beginning to fill the tables and make their way toward the bar. The din started picking up, slowly drowning out the soft music playing in the background. That was about what he expected, and once all the formalities and speeches were over, he knew it would only get louder. After, would come the dinner, and then everyone would start drinking in earnest, assured that all would be well once they had a full stomach to soak it up.

General Nito glanced at David from a few feet away. Nito was one of the generals David had been slowly trying to convince to shift Philip away from his current position. It was an odd situation, as Nito was on good terms with Philip and David, and to lean one way or the other would show preference. Much like himself, Nito preferred to stay out of the political games of their fellows if he could help it, which made the situation even more delicate.

"A little worried, David?" Nito asked with a crooked smile.

David shook his head. "Nothing to be concerned about. Everything is completely under control."

Nito chuckled. "I remember last year—"

"And the year before, and the year before that," David added with a grimace.

The year before, the DJ mysteriously disappeared halfway through the Gala. It had taken more than an hour to hunt the man down. David was not a man known for his temper, but he had lashed out when he found out the DJ had been discovered in an unused room, apparently having a private party with a couple of female privates equipped with a booze and cocaine supply. David had never enjoyed having to punish privates personally and making sure someone was fired as he'd had to do that night.

Nito's eyes slid to the tables being set up for the food. "No food poisoning this year, right?"

That had been the year before last, and David didn't need the reminder. He still couldn't figure out if that had been an accident, one of those things that happened, or a mistake on the catering company's part. He hadn't hired that company since, just to be sure, but the memory of a quarter of the attendees ending up violently ill was burned in his mind.

David frowned at him. "Everything is under control this year. We will not have any incidents."

Nito chuckled. "You sure?"

"Yes."

And he was, completely. Along with running an entire base, the added stress of juggling the gala arrangement usually left him fumbling. The same added stress had been thrown into the hands of previous assistants he'd had, with mixed and typically disastrous results.

"This year, I have help, and a great deal of it," David said.

"That so? And you didn't before?"

"Not quite like this. My current assistant is very capable and has done a great deal to alleviate the burden on me."

"You've always had an assistant."

"This one is different."

Nito hummed thoughtfully. "The others weren't quite up to snuff then?"

David chuckled. "They were capable, well, most of them were anyway. However, this one is above and beyond and very dedicated to ensuring everything is done precisely."

He had yet to catch sight of Christian, though he had received a message from the younger man when he'd arrived. It had been followed by more messages, updating David on everything Christian was up to and what he was focusing on. It brought him no small amusement to think of Christian out of sight, checking every little detail.

"So, no problems then," Nito said.

David shook his head. "None to report."

Then again, he suspected Christian wouldn't pass them along. In David's experience, he tackled problems head-on rather than bring them to David's attention. Only when Christian was unable to think of a solution on his own, or because of his lack of authority or access, did he bring the problem to David. Sometimes, David worried that Christian was taking too much on himself, but he couldn't argue with the results.

"Well, everything certainly seems to be moving smoothly so far. I will give you and your *wunderkind* that," Nito said with a glance around the spacious room.

"I agree. I can't say I have any fault to find."

"And it certainly looks grander than usual in here. Were the rugs meant to give the idea of the sea, or was that accidental?"

David smirked. "Intentional."

And the green cloth covering the tables, hemmed with a tawny brown, were intentionally meant to give the idea of little islands. It was a far more subtle idea than the god-awful tropical theme the year before.

"Whose?"

"My assistant, of course. Christian has an eye for that sort of thing."

"Oh, on a first-name basis, are you?"

David forced a smile, cursing himself inwardly. "The man has been at my side for almost a year now. A certain level of familiarity and camaraderie is to be expected."

"True, though I don't think I've heard you refer to any of your former assistants so informally."

"None of them have been quite as remarkable."

"Well, if what you say is true, this one is certainly worth keeping around."

David looked sidelong at his friend. "Please tell me you aren't about to start fishing for his transfer to your office."

Nito laughed. "No, no, I won't poach your precious assistant. And if he's as dedicated to his job as it sounds, it would be poaching too. I can't imagine I could convince him to transfer willingly."

"No, you couldn't," David said with a knowing smile.

Nito looked around. "Speaking of casual, where is Philip?"

David kept a straight face. "I believe he is currently entertaining the other esteemed guests in a private room. I'm sure they will show up within the hour."

"Half-drunk just in time for your speech."

"Undoubtedly."

"Good that Philip is doing his part."

David nodded but said nothing. In truth, he should have been able to rely on Philip more than Christian for the arrangements. While Philip's job description centered around the base's operations, it should have also included setting up the Gala. Oh, sure, Philip had sent him a long list of ideas and suggestions, but most of them had been absurdly expensive and ostentatious. There was no need to bring in the best of the best, from decorators to food companies, just for the Gala. The Gala was a show, of course, and it was meant to display what Fort Dale had to offer while also providing a night of socializing, fun, and free refreshments.

The problem, as so often with Philip, lay in what was considered important. David had tried to understand that, for Philip, the importance of his duties and job lay in good presentation. After all, Command really only cared if things went wrong, with only the occasional notice of an exemplary job well done. But it had begun to wear on David's nerves, whose duty, in his mind, was to take care of the men and women in his charge. Those viewpoints rarely found common ground, and David couldn't wait to get Philip out of his hair and into a position where he would be far more comfortable and flourish.

"As well as he can," David finally said.

Nito eyed him, snorting softly. "Don't think I haven't forgotten our previous conversation."

"I wasn't attempting to remind you, either. If I wanted to do that, I would say so...admittedly, not here and now."

"No, I suppose not. I'm still giving it thought."

David looked around, realizing he should socialize before

the Gala officially started. It was one of the few things about the evening he enjoyed. Stuck in his office as often as he was or on calls and in meetings, he very rarely had the chance to meet the soldiers he was in charge of. For them, the Gala was a social event to be enjoyed and soaked up, and it meant he saw them at their most relaxed. It was the one way he knew he was doing something right.

"By all means, give it thought, and then even more. Meanwhile, I am going to attend to my social duties," David said, setting his glass aside to step down from the dais.

"Have fun. I'm going to continue drinking quietly in a corner."

"I'll consider doing the same *after* the speech," David said.

* * *

DAVID LEANED, practically sagging over the bar as he eyed the trio of bartenders. He had to admit, there was something hypnotic about watching the three men as they dodged, weaved, and swerved around one another with little more than the occasional word of warning.

When he finally caught one's attention, he ordered himself a whiskey, double if they would, on the rocks. His entire speech had gone off without a hitch and with the same predictable pattern. Open with a greeting to all in attendance, bring special attention to the higher-ups who'd come, and begin the magnanimous speech that applauded the efforts and successes of Fort Dale. It was nothing special, and the only difference between each year's speech was the detail of the achievements. He made sure to keep it short, knowing damn well no one came to the Gala to listen to him drone on. Speeches weren't his forte, but despite memorizing most of the speech, he always walked away tense and with a dry throat.

"Thank you," he said as he was handed his glass within seconds.

It wasn't the whiskey he kept in his private supply but damned if that first sip of liquor wasn't the most welcome sensation he'd had all night. He turned his gaze to the rest of the hall, watching as the meals were brought to the tables, along with drink orders. It had been Christian's idea to spend a little extra and bring in servers for the drinks to prevent the inevitable traffic jam with large groups and an open bar.

David frowned, realizing he hadn't seen Christian all night. It made sense when Christian was busy running around behind the scenes, keeping the details neat and orderly, while David kept to the front of the house. But he would have expected the younger man to have appeared by the time the food was served, but he had not seen a glimpse of that familiar blond head.

Taking his glass with him, he walked around the large room. His eyes darted left and right, looking at tables where people stood talking. Though he checked everyone, David's worry deepened as he never once spotted Christian. He made another circuit, waving and greeting people, but still couldn't find him. Messages from Christian had stopped shortly before the start of the speech, so David had no idea where the man had disappeared.

Slipping through the door behind the catering tables, David stepped into the noisy kitchen. Mindful that he could get in the way, he stayed to the edge as he looked around and again found nothing.

One of the passing chefs looked up. "Everything alright?"

"Looking for someone," David said.

The man frowned. "If you're looking for the slave driver, he said something about getting some air."

David chuckled. "I see things have been interesting."

The man grunted, turning away with what sounded like muttered curses. Smiling, David exited through the side door and into the hallway. He knew the building well, having had to host an annual Gala and other smaller functions, but its main purpose was to feed the soldiers on the base. He didn't get to visit casually as often as he would like, but he'd done it enough for over a decade to know the layout.

Which meant he also had a good idea where Christian had disappeared to.

Moving further from the sound of the party, David mounted the stairs at the end of the hallway. The second floor was used for smaller parties or important meetings that couldn't be done in his office. At the far end, one of the rooms had a balcony that looked out over the sea. It was his favorite place to take special guests, though usually only for events that required a certain degree of sobriety.

Walking swiftly down the carpeted hallway, he found the door at the end of the hall open a crack. Pushing it wide, he stepped into the dimly lit room. The plush couches and armchairs sat in the moonlight, streaming through the open double doors at the back of the room. A shadow moved, a man shifting position and bending to lean on the rail surrounding the balcony.

Smiling, David walked forward, lips parting to greet Christian softly. He stopped just short of the doorway as he caught sight of the man, words dying before they reached his lips.

Christian stood, bent over, his elbows resting on the stone rail. The young man was looking out at the ocean, though the distant look in his eyes said he wasn't actually seeing the scenery. Half his face was hidden, but the half he could see looked irritated and worn out. Christian's hair had grown out enough that David could see it was in disarray, little tufts sticking up as though Christian had been running his hands through it. There was a line of cooling sweat at his temple and a black smudge along his cheek. His uniform was askew, the collar open to reveal a once pristine, now stained, white shirt beneath it. The moonlight caught the blond scruff of his five o'clock shadow, completing the look. No doubt, Christian would say he looked an absolute mess.

To David, Christian was breathtaking.

Christian frowned, turning to face him with a sharp jerk. His blue eyes were shadowed as he turned from the moonlight. His bunched shoulders eased when he saw David standing in the room, a soft sound escaping him.

"Oh, it's you," Christian said.

"Sorry to disappoint?" David wondered.

Christian snorted. "Not at all. I thought it was someone from the catering company coming to find me again. They've been up my ass from the moment I told them I was the one to come to."

"I met one of the chefs. He wasn't a fan of yours, it sounded like," David chuckled.

Christian's lip curled. "The service people needed constant handholding, but the chefs weren't even ready for tonight. They forgot the cabbage. How the hell do you forget cabbage when you're serving a dish that focuses on cabbage? I had to go out and buy a shit ton of cabbage and drag it back here, and then they bitched about the damn quality. Well, excuse the fuck out of me. Maybe you should have been *professionals* and brought your own damn supply!"

David's brow raised as he stepped forward. He'd never seen Christian frustrated enough to swear or let such heat into his voice. It only added to the impression that Christian had been worn down from the past couple of hours and the oddly alluring effect it had on him. David leaned on the railing beside Christian, watching him.

"And then, the damn servers forgot their assigned tables

and couldn't get the orders right. I had to dig through the files I'd passed to the company *months ago* to find what we decided on. So, I had to find a way to print them off and ensure everyone knew where they were supposed to be and when. It's honestly a goddamn miracle something didn't go wrong with the bartenders. The worst they had was running low on ice, and thankfully, there's a whole fuck ton of it in the storage freezers they could chip at."

David watched Christian's eyes light up as he scowled at the ocean. David had no doubt at least a dozen or more things were flying through Christian's mind. One box ticked off after another on the list of grievances. He had seen Christian at work as a professional. He had seen him half-drunk, bashful, and craving touch. Now, he was seeing Christian when he'd hit his limit of patience and understanding, when anger and frustration boiled out in a hot stream of furious words.

Christian glanced at him. "What?"

"I'm just listening to you," David said quietly.

Christian took a deep breath, grimacing. "I know. I'm sorry. I said I'd take care of this so you wouldn't have to, but I honestly did not expect everything to go wrong like it did. I'm...just frustrated at the moment. I swear, I'm okay."

David nodded. "I know you will be."

"I just wanted this Gala to go right without any disasters."

David smiled. "And I'd say you managed that with flying colors."

"Yeah, except now I'm the disaster."

David reached out, taking his thumb, damp from the condensation on his glass, and wiping at the black smudge on Christian's cheek. It came off easily, but his touch lingered on Christian's handsome face. David curled his fingers to cup his cheek, a soft smile on his lips as Christian leaned willingly into the touch.

"You're anything but a disaster right now," David told him.

"I feel like one."

David set his glass aside, wiping his palm clean so he could take the other side of Christian's face in his hand. He turned the man's face, his gaze sweeping over him as Christian's frustration melted. It was replaced by cautious hope and gratitude as he continued to accept David's touch, half-closing his eyes at the comfort.

"Feeling like a disaster isn't the same as being one. You went above and beyond what I expected of you tonight and succeeded. I'm sure quite a few more things, big and small, happened tonight to bring you out here, away from seeing the fruits of your labors. Frustration is to be expected."

Christian smiled. "Thank you, David."

Hearing his name instead of his title from Christian's mouth sent David's heart pounding against his ribs. Smiling, he ran a thumb over the younger man's lips. David knew what he'd told Christian, that he'd needed time to think things over, to consider the risks and rewards. But he was beginning to realize that if David didn't take the chance, didn't take what Christian was offering now, someone else might come along and take him up on it instead.

"Stay with me tonight?" David asked softly.

Christian's eyes widened. "What?"

"After this is over, and we've sent everyone on their way. Come back, stay in my bed...with me."

Christian's eyes darted all over David's face, searching. "But you—"

David nodded. "I know."

Unable to bear waiting any longer, he leaned forward to kiss him. As soon as their lips met, David didn't regret his sudden decision for a moment. The heat he'd felt the first time he'd taken the initiative and kissed the hopeful Christian returned in full force. More important than the lust beginning to bubble in his gut was the happiness he felt as Christian melted against him, relaxing completely.

"We'll talk," David whispered against his lips.

"Tonight," Christian confirmed.

"Tonight."

CHRISTIAN

Floating peacefully in a sea of warmth and mindlessness, Christian let out a soft groan of protest. He'd been so content lying against the comforting press of David's huge, plush bed. David's arm was thrown over his waist, curled up to press his hand against Christian's chest and hold him in place. He was vaguely aware of all of it and would have been content to lay there forever, basking in the presence of David's body flush against his, the warmth of their shared body heat beneath the blankets, and the peace of sleep.

Except for the damn sunlight hitting his face.

Christian groaned again, rolling away from the window and the accursed light. Instead, he pressed his face against David's chest and held it there with a grumble of complaint. It was followed by a low, rumbling chuckle echoing from David's chest as he adjusted his hold on Christian, keeping him close.

"Good morning," David said, voice rough with sleep.

"Would be good if the sun would go away," Christian muttered.

"It won't go away from this side of the house for a good few hours," David told him.

"That's the worst thing I've heard this morning."

"Then let me make it better by saying you're adorable when you wake up."

Christian paused, then smiled. "Okay, that made it better."

"Good."

He was content to lie there a little longer, still greedily soaking up the heat of David's body. Neither had been ready to follow through on David's promise when they'd stumbled through his door the night before. The Gala had wiped Christian out, and he'd sensed David wasn't much better off. The most they could manage was to pull their clothes off and stumble into bed, Christian still wearing his underwear and one sock. In contrast, David, at least, managed to get completely naked.

A few hours later, Christian woke up to a familiar thick presence pressing against his back, and he found he had a little more energy. David had woken a few minutes before him and taken to stroking Christian's body tenderly, trying not to wake him. Christian wasn't sure if it had been the light touches that had brought him awake or the man's bare cock pushing against his back. Either way, he'd been more than happy to roll over and pounce, eager to feel his cock inside him again.

And now he was wrapped in the man's arms, his body still a little tender but happy and wondering what was going to happen. He had to believe something good was coming his way after the night's events. Christian couldn't believe David would kiss him, promise they'd talk, and then spend the night like they were lovers for nothing.

Christian grunted. "Great, now I'm awake."

David chuckled, rubbing a hand over Christian's lower back. "That's what happens when you wake up."

"Yes, I always wondered about that."

"Smartass."

"Tender ass, more like it," Christian grunted.

David leaned back to peer down at him. "Really? I thought I was pretty gentle last night."

"In comparison to the first time, yeah."

"Oh. I'm sorry."

Christian chuckled, kissing David quickly. "Don't be. That wasn't a complaint. Plus, no amount of lube and gentleness can completely take away from the friction of a condom after a little while. Well, and you're the first person I've slept with in months...my body isn't exactly used to it."

"Well, maybe we should do something about that," David said.

Christian raised a brow. "Yeah?"

David smiled. "Why don't I make us some coffee, and you and I can talk like I promised."

"This isn't going to be a...bad talk or anything, is it?" Christian asked as his nerves finally got the better of him.

David leaned forward, kissing Christian's forehead. "I certainly hope not."

He wasn't sure what that meant, but Christian would accept it. David wasn't a man who rushed into anything and erred more toward heavy thought than immediate action. In truth, Christian had expected him to take far longer than a few days to come to a conclusion, and he wondered what had changed that patient habit.

"Alright, but I'm the one making the coffee. I don't trust your non-coffee-drinking ass to make it," Christian said, wriggling out of David's grip.

"Someone's eager," David said with a smirk.

Christian hopped off the bed and stretched. "You promised me coffee. Once you offer me coffee, I want it immediately."

David rolled onto his back, eyes roving Christian's naked body greedily. "By all means, help yourself. I wasn't going to make any for myself anyway."

"Ooh, so I get to make it my way?"

"That you do."

"Yes!"

Christian almost skipped toward the kitchen, where the delicious brew of the Gods waited. However, he hesitated as he watched David take his turn to stretch before getting out of bed. Christian's groin stirred as he watched the man's well-cared-for body on full display in the invading sunlight. Dark hair glistened on his stomach in a thin but bold line, and Christian could see just a peek of the dark hair that rested above the man's cock. He knew all too well what the blanket was hiding, and for a moment, he was tempted to dive back onto the bed and help himself again.

David snorted, pointing to the kitchen. "Weren't you about to make coffee?"

"What, like you weren't just checking me out?"

"With an ass like that, how could I not?"

"And when you look as good as you do, all sleepy and sexy in bed, how can I not do the same?"

David smiled. "Because you have coffee to attend to. And afterward, we should probably take a shower."

"To get clean or to get dirty all over again?"

"I suppose that depends on you, doesn't it?"

Knowing he was dismissed, Christian turned on his heel, still grinning, and marched out of the room. Once more, he found his mind wondering what David would say. Christian wasn't foolish enough to believe that he and David being something, dating seriously, and maybe falling in love wouldn't be dangerous. The two of them were more than a couple of decades apart, and in reality, their positions made a romance very dangerous for both of them.

Yet, his mind couldn't help but fixate on their few moments together. Something about being with David felt *right*. Some part of him, his heart, if Christian wanted to be romantic, felt at home in David's arms. The sex was mind-blowing, their conversations came easily, and they knew they could depend on one another when the going got tough. Maybe there were plenty of reasons to avoid a romantic relationship, but Christian also thought there were plenty of reasons to stick with it.

As he rummaged around to find the coffee, he felt an arm wrap around his waist and pull him back suddenly. Startled from his thoughts, Christian let out a small yelp as he felt his back collide with David's front. He laughed softly as David's other arm wrapped around his chest, keeping him in place so he couldn't wriggle away.

"David! I'm trying to make coffee like you ordered," Christian protested.

"And I come out of my room, finding you bent over in my kitchen. How could I resist?"

The growl in David's voice was no longer because he was half-asleep. Oh no, Christian could hear the man was wide awake, and that was all desire in his rough voice. And if his voice wasn't an indication, the press of David's cock into his back certainly was.

Christian shivered. "We're not making it to the shower first, are we?"

"No."

With that simple word, Christian melted into David's arms. Only then did he realize one of David's hands was not gripping him but something else. A low gasp broke from him as he saw the familiar bottle of lube and the shiny wrapper of a condom.

"Damn, you came prepared," Christian murmured, turning his head to kiss David as best he could.

"I might have gone back and grabbed what we needed," David told him.

Christian succeeded in his attempt to kiss David, moaning softly as their lips parted. An idea blossomed in his head, and while he knew it was probably a bad idea to bring it up, he couldn't help himself.

"Do you trust me?" Christian heard himself ask.

David pulled back, raising a brow. "Of course I do."

"No," Christian began, reaching down to pull the condom from David's grasp. "Do you *trust* me?"

David's eyes lit up in understanding, his brow falling to a frown. "You...want to go without?"

It was one hell of a question to ask, considering he still didn't know if they would be something serious. Yet, he knew damn well he trusted David to be honest with him if going bare was safe. On the one hand, he desperately wanted that display of pure trust between them and, hopefully, foreshadowing what would come when they finally talked. On the other hand, a far hornier side of his mind wanted to feel the general's bare cock and to feel him come inside him.

"If you think we can," Christian said.

David's bottom lip caught between his teeth. "It's been...a while since I went without."

Christian chuckled nervously. "I've never."

David's eyes widened. "What?"

"I've never gone bare before."

He knew enough about going bare to know it felt better for both partners, and there tended to be less irritation for the person who received. Christian had always wanted to feel someone's bare cock inside him, to know what it felt like to be bonded, skin to skin. Still, he'd never trusted a partner enough. He did not give trust easily, even though he tried to find the best in people. He would not throw away his health on a fling or a short-term boyfriend.

But for David? He'd do it in a heartbeat.

"Feels like that should be for a more special moment than me fucking you on a counter," David said, eyes darting between Christian and the condom.

Christian laughed. "Are you kidding me? Just having you inside me is going to be romantic enough."

David's pupils swelled, but his grin returned. "A man of simple tastes."

"And easy to please," Christian told him.

David released him, taking the condom and tossing it absently onto the counter. The bottle of lube, however, was opened and placed nearby. Christian hummed happily a moment later when he was pulled into a hungry kiss, now facing David. It required him to stand on the tips of his toes to reach the man's lips comfortably, but he considered it well worth it.

He jumped when he felt cold fingers, covered in lube, find their way to his hole. Christian wasn't sure when David managed to coat his fingers, but he knew he could be pretty sneaky when he wanted. Instead, he moaned as the first digit slipped into him, sliding in and lubing his insides. A moment later, a second finger joined the first, drawing a low chuckle from him.

"Something funny?" David asked as he spread his fingers apart.

Christian grunted. "Just how patient you usually are with everything, but when it comes to sex, you've got zero patience."

A third finger probed him as David grinned. "Maybe it's your effect. Problem?"

Christian moaned as the third finger spread him open, making him clutch onto David harder. "God, no."

"Good," David murmured as he pushed his fingers deeper.

The tenderness from the night before was quickly lost as

David's fingers found the right place deep inside him. Christian arched his back, giving in almost immediately to the demands of David's hands on him. As much as he loved to tease and taunt the older man in their everyday lives, it was perfect giving in to David when he wanted Christian so plainly that he felt the need to claim him on the spot.

David broke the kiss, whispering harshly against his lips. "Lean on the counter, spread your legs."

"Fuck," Christian muttered.

But he didn't argue. Extracting himself from David's grip, he turned and did as he was told. In truth, he would have probably bent over double if David had ordered him to and would have gripped his ankles with a smile. Thankfully, he needed only to lean over the cool countertop and spread his legs, knowing he was putting himself on full display.

He didn't have to wait long for David to take advantage. A hand came to rest on his lower back, pinning his hips against the counter with a firm hold. Christian looked over his shoulder, a shiver running through him when he caught David's pale eyes locked on him as he moved forward. The next moment, he felt the blunt head of the man's cock pressing against him.

And then, he opened for him. Christian bowed his head, moaning softly as he felt David's cock slide into his stretched hole. He wasn't sure if it was smoother because David had taken the time to open him, the fact that they hadn't gone that long without sex, or the lack of a condom, or some combination of the three. What he did know was it felt absolutely amazing.

"Damn," David hissed as he eased in halfway.

"Agreed," Christian said with a shaky voice.

David's cock still had to spread him wide. His fingers hadn't done the job completely. Christian relished the feeling of the man's cock sliding into him, filling him so much his body was forced to adjust. There was almost no burn this time, just the sensation of David, unimpeded and uncovered, moving deep into him. He would swear he could feel the man's heartbeat without the condom, and his cock was already straining.

Christian was pressed harder against the counter when David reared back and slid into him again with a grunt. Christian didn't need to be told to keep still as he felt David's grip on his hips tighten, nails digging into his skin. It didn't stop him from arching his back, though, or the wanton moans escaping his lips as David thrust into him again and again.

Skin met skin with a sharp slap each time David bottomed out, hitting Christian deeply and dragging desperate sounds from him. Never had he known sex to start so smoothly and escalate so rapidly into pure pleasure. He was never gladder that David's house was far from the other buildings on base as he cried out with each thrust.

"Stamina isn't going to be so good this time," David warned.

Excitement, unlike any other, zinged through Christian with the force of a lightning bolt at those words. Eagerness took over, and he found himself pushing his hips back into David's thrusts as best as he could. No longer just there for the ride, Christian wanted to feel David come, wanted to feel him explode deep inside him.

"Christian," David hissed.

"Oh, *please*, do it."

David's grip on his hips redoubled, and the man thrust hard. The next thrust was just as brutal, pinning Christian against the counter as David hammered against him, getting as deep as possible on each thrust. He felt him stiffen, shoving hard one final time and letting out a deep growl.

Christian moaned as he could *feel* the twitch of David's

cock. Warmth flooded his ass as David came deep, his hips pushing against him with every spurt. It was too much for Christian, knowing it was *David* inside him, coming deep. Christian let out a low cry, sagging as he felt his release wash through him, painting the front of the counter.

David panted, his hands firmly on Christian as he held him steady. "Did you just—"

"Yep, hands-free. Oh, holy shit," Christian said breathlessly.

He felt himself yanked up forcefully, his head turned to be kissed fiercely by David. Christian moaned as he felt their kiss force David's cock to twist and twitch inside him. Even post-orgasm, he never felt a twinge of regret, glad it was David he had waited for before he'd taken the plunge.

"You are too much fun," David whispered.

"One of my many talents," Christian said.

David chuckled, stroking Christian's face. "I guess we should see about that shower now."

"When I can walk right, sure."

David said nothing, a playful smirk on his face as he gently eased out of Christian. For a minute, Christian thought he was going to let him drop to the ground before he felt himself hoisted into the air. He flailed, instinctively wrapping his arms around David's neck and squeezing. He was safe, however, cradled in David's arms as the older man turned toward the bedroom.

"I've got you covered," David said with a grin.

Christian laughed as he was carried through the house. "You know, your dick didn't cripple me."

"Well, that's a relief."

"But I'm not going to argue with being carried either."

"Good, because we're almost to the shower anyway."

Christian leaned up, kissing the corner of David's mouth. "My hero, saving me from my wobbly legs."

"Well, I wobbled them, so I might as well do the rest."

Christian laughed, feeling a little high. There was no way David would have gone bare with him if he wasn't prepared to make something more of the two of them. Christian knew he had chosen the right person to give himself to completely, and his stomach fluttered as he thought of having more mornings like this and more nights like the one before. Everything was falling into place for them, and he couldn't be happier.

A sharp knock echoed through the house, killing Christian's laugh.

"What was that?" Christian asked.

David's eyes shifted toward the front of the house, frowning. "The front door."

DAVID

Still frowning, he gently placed Christian on the tiled floor of his bathroom. "Stay here."

"Yeah, I'm just going to go answer your door butt naked," Christian said.

David frowned but sensed the tension in Christian and left it alone. Instead, he turned and grabbed the lounge pants and t-shirt he'd laid out the day before and had never worn to bed. The knocking came again, just as insistent and demanding, drawing David's brow even tighter.

Who the hell would be trying to break his door down?

David wasn't used to having visitors at home. The only people who'd seen his house were family and a few friends. David never hosted guests at his house, and it was pretty well known that he did not welcome surprise visitors. It was something he'd established early on when he'd come to Fort Dale. His home was his sanctuary, a fortress against the rest of the world. He didn't care if it was still technically on base. If someone wanted him while he was home, they could use the damn phone like any normal person.

Reaching the front door, he pulled aside the curtain curiously. His frown deepened when he saw who stood on the other side of the door. Sighing, he pinched his brow and waved at Christian, who he could see peeking through the bedroom door. No, Christian could not show himself.

David opened the door, a frown set on his face. "Philip, what a surprise."

The plump man beamed up at him. "David, a pleasure."

A sentiment David didn't share, but he wasn't going to express that fact. Philip could be notoriously bad-tempered when he was made to feel like an annoyance or wasn't welcome. David couldn't remember ever knowing someone as sensitive and yet so utterly blind to social convention as Philip.

David forced a smile on his face. "I can't say I was expecting anyone to visit. Normally, the day after the Gala is the day we all take off."

Philip nodded vigorously. "Of course, of course. No doubt, you're tired after the night you had. I had a hard time getting out of bed, but business calls, and I have to answer."

David's frown returned. "Business? You have the day off, Philip."

Philip's smile turned chilly. "Yes, I think you and I should talk. A few things to...iron out."

David's mental hackles rose, and he slowly cocked his head. "Is that so? Well, since I have the day off too, and since it doesn't sound like an emergency, you can visit me at the office."

Despite the alarm bells going off in his head, David would be damned before he let himself be walked over and have his house invaded by Philip *that* easily.

"I think you might want to hear what I have to say," Philip said with the same smile.

"I'm not sure I like the way you're speaking to me, Philip.

We've been on good terms for a while now, but you're beginning to test my patience," David warned.

"Then maybe your boy toy would like to hear what I have to say."

David went cold. "Excuse me?"

"I wanted to speak to both of you. I stopped by his place first, but he didn't appear to be home. So, it only makes sense that he's here," Philip said, with the air of someone talking about the weather.

"Is that so?" David asked in a tight voice.

Philip brushed a non-existent speck of dirt from his collar. "Yes. Let's not insult our intelligence, David. Obviously, I know about you and Christian, and I want to speak to you about that. Now, I want this to be a friendly affair. Please don't make this harder than it needs to be."

David's face fell into a stony indifference as he considered what to do. Philip didn't appear to want to cause a fuss, which could be a good thing. Or it could be bad, depending on what the other man had in mind. However, inviting him into his house made David uneasy, especially since Christian *was* there and would hear everything. David wasn't sure if he wanted to admit outright Christian was there, but he might as well play along for a while.

"I'd be very interested to hear what you have to say. Why don't you come in, Philip? I was getting ready to make coffee," David said, stepping back from the door.

"And here I thought you didn't drink coffee," Philip said as he stepped into the house after him.

David shrugged. "I've been known to partake now and again. But I do have the occasional guest here, and they enjoy the coffee. So I keep a stock just in case."

"Ah, yes, I'm sure you've had a great many guests here."

David tensed as he began to fiddle with the machine. "The

only guests I've ever had in my home are my family and dear friends."

"Ah, well, Christian should feel very special being allowed to come here then," Philip said as he sat at one of the bar stools.

David flipped on the machine with a snort. "Forgive me, Philip. I know you're an intelligent man, so you can understand my reluctance to understand where this sudden theory of my and Christian's supposed relationship came from."

Philip's smile turned greedy. "Well, I'll admit, it came as a bit of a surprise to me. I mean, I knew you enjoyed a bit of young flesh and all, but I never expected you to be so bold as to pursue the man who worked your front desk. I was...shocked when I discovered that."

"You continue to speak but provide me with nothing, Philip. Make your case, or get the hell out of my house," David said.

Philip chuckled. "You can't intimidate me, David. You and I have known each other for far too long for that 'Dad' look to work on me."

"Then you should know I don't like my time wasted."

"Then I'll stop wasting it," Philip said as he reached into his pockets.

David watched Philip pull out his phone and place it on the counter. Stepping forward, David picked up the device and felt the floor to his stomach fall out. Clear as day was a picture of him and Christian standing on the balcony overlooking the sea. Whoever had taken the photo had been standing below them and had obviously been using good equipment. The image was close and clear enough to make out exactly who they were and to see their lips pressed against one another as David tried to comfort the younger man.

"My, that is quite an interesting picture you have, Philip. I never knew you were into photography," David said, feeling lightheaded.

"Oh, only certain pictures, and I'm terrible at taking them. But if you have the money, you can always pay someone else to take them for you," Philip said, reaching to take the phone back.

David let the device go, knowing that breaking it wouldn't matter. "Ah, I see. You hired someone to follow me and take pictures?"

Philip nodded, pocketing the device. "Yes, you see, I've known about your predilection for young men, and I thought that was an important detail to remember. What I didn't count on was just how careful you would be. You never allowed yourself any public displays before this, nothing that could be used. I mean, I could have made a case from a few, but I needed something a little more substantial."

David didn't have to think too hard about who Philip was considering contacting. "For Command."

Philip tapped the counter with a wink. "Right on the head."

David's stomach turned as he realized Philip was more than happy to present that picture to Command, given half a reason. And yet—

"You haven't gone to them," David pointed out.

Philip sighed. "I honestly thought I was never going to get my chance. Everything I had wasn't going to count for much. I mean, Command is a stickler for a good image, and while you talking or visiting younger men wouldn't have been enough to offend the old guard in control right now, it would have hinted. I didn't want a hint, though. I didn't want a sliver of a chance."

"Of what?" David asked between gritted teeth.

"Of you to get out of it. You're a clever man, David, inspiring confidence and goodwill in others. The last thing I needed was for you to use all the good ol' boy charm to wriggle your way out. I thought I had something before, and then it mysteriously slipped from my grasp. I'd almost given up hope, and then this hit my email this morning, and I couldn't be more delighted."

Christian appeared in the doorway, dressed, his jaw tight. "Ethan."

Philip's eyes brightened, turning on his stool to face Christian. "Ah, Christian, it's good to see you."

Christian scowled. "No point in bothering with the friendly act. You're the one who put Ethan up to the blackmail."

Philip blinked. "Blunt, I see why you and David get along so well. Though, blackmail? Ah, now I'm beginning to understand."

And so was David. "You contacted Ethan. You wanted the video and pictures he had, didn't you?"

"Well, I knew you'd been with him for a while. And despite not getting anything worthwhile on my end, I was...curious to see if he had anything I could use. He swore up and down he did. I promised him a great deal for it, and he seemed quite eager. That was until suddenly it was mysteriously gone," Philip finished with a frown.

David chuckled mirthlessly. "You trusted the wrong person. He tried blackmailing me first. For money."

Philip laughed softly. "I see, I see. The little shit tried to get money from both of us then. To see who he could get the larger amount from?"

"Or to get the money from me and hand it over to get money from you as well," David growled.

"Tricky. I should give him a job. Except for the part where he failed," Philip said with a haughty sniff.

David looked up at Christian, who was still standing behind Philip, glowering furiously at him. David had thought it strange that despite having had the evidence for a while, Ethan had sat on it until recently. Apparently, it had never occurred to the younger man how damning his evidence was until Philip contacted him. If it hadn't been for Christian, David might have ended up screwed anyway.

Philip followed his gaze, turning to Christian. "Did *you* have something to do with that?"

Christian crossed his arms over his chest. "You didn't come here to tell us you knew about us, just to have fun. If you wanted to remove David, you would have sent everything you had to Command and let them do the dirty work for you."

"True," Philip said, nodding.

"So, what do you want?" David asked.

Philip winked. "Easy. Step down."

David reeled. "Excuse me?"

"All you need to do is resign. The trials of running this base have been too much for you over the years, and you crave something a little less demanding. I'm sure they will undoubtedly place you somewhere nice, and hey, with your kind words in my favor, they can put me in your position instead," Philip said, steepling his fingers in front of him.

David stared. "You want me to essentially hand over my position as head of Fort Dale to you? On a platter?"

"Well, it's either that or I hand over everything to Command and let them do what they will. Now, I don't know about you, but I don't think they'll be kind. They might be willing to overlook all the other boy toys, but Christian? You'll be crucified. And I doubt Christian will come out unscathed," Philip said with the politest of smiles.

"You son of a bitch," David growled, stepping forward.

Christian rounded the counter, not looking at Philip. "Hey, don't. Don't give him a reason."

"And before you get any smart ideas, all my evidence is stored in several places. Well, and if anything...untoward should happen to me, know that my...friend is instructed to hand over everything," Philip continued, unfazed by David's outburst.

"You think I'd try to have you killed?" David asked in disbelief.

"You are a noble and honorable man, David, but nothing fights harder than a wounded, cornered animal," Philip said simply.

Christian shook his head. "David, don't. I-I can do this."

David looked down at him, frowning. "What? Do what?"

Christian smiled. "It won't be too hard to spin them a tale of woe and troubles. I can tell them I was the one who kissed you, that you were very kind about the whole thing and never let it go any further. You've been a good general, leader, and mentor, and I was the one who went too far."

Philip scowled, "Noble, but that's hardly going to work."

Christian smirked. "If it wasn't, you wouldn't look so irritated."

David turned Christian to face him, shaking his head. "Like hell. You're not ruining your life for this, no."

"What are they going to do? Kick out someone who was already thinking about getting out anyway?"

"And get your record ruined for it?"

"It's better than you, who would get his entire career ruined because some pompous douche couldn't get the job right."

Philip cleared his throat. "I am still sitting right here."

Christian turned a glare toward him. "I'm aware."

David shook his head again. "No, Christian, no. You don't need to go to bat for me again, especially when it *would* ruin everything."

Christian smiled. "And how would you stop me?"

David chuckled, tapping Christian's cheek lightly. "Because you don't need to."

"They'll tear you apart."

David hummed. "I know. I'll probably end up demoted, losing my position. I might be lucky enough not to get a discharge, but I'd be tainted for the rest of my career. Which is more than I can say for Philip."

Philip looked back at him, confusion on his face. "Pardon?"

David gently pushed Christian away to face the pudgy man. "October 2nd, 2011."

Philip's eyes widened, face going pale. "You...you didn't."

David tilted his head, barely contained glee in his voice. "I did."

Christian looked between them. "I'm...confused."

David held Philip's gaze. "October 2nd, 2011. Philip had been transferred to Fort Dale only a couple of months beforehand. It was covertly made known to me that he came with a few...problems but that they shouldn't be a problem. That was, until the 2nd. See, Philip here had a bit of a party problem."

Philip's face flushed. "You said you'd taken care of it."

"I never lied. I took care of the problem and swept everything under the rug. I never said I erased everything, though," David shot back.

"Uh, please tell me this doesn't involve a dead hooker," Christian said with a nervous glance toward David.

"Not even I would have covered that up. But it does involve a hooker, a few actually, quite alive. And it also involves Philip with them and enough cocaine to fuel a week-long bender between the four of them," David explained.

Christian blinked. "Uh, three...hookers?"

"Three. I'll spare you the intimate details, but I'm not the only one foolish enough to allow someone to bring a camera. And unlike me, Philip got caught, not by someone snooping or trying to blackmail him, but because he'd made such an awful fuss that the hotel had no choice but to call the police. So here's the man in charge of operations, caught with hookers, enough sex toys to open a shop, and cocaine."

Christian whistled. "Damn, Phil, you, uh, really knew how to have a good time."

"You should have seen him the following day in my office, after I got him out of jail. It was a pitiful sight, and I, like an idiot, took pity on him. It took a great deal of convincing and pulling a few favors, but we had the whole thing swept under the rug. Philip promised to behave, and all was good."

"Until now," Christian added.

"You're lying. You don't have shit," Philip finally hissed.

"Oh, I have *everything*. Want to know what I had to pay the hotel for them to hand over the footage from that night? Do you want to revisit all those pictures? I still have the camera one lovely lady was willing to give me, so long as I gave her enough money to live off while she found a much safer job."

Christian looked at Philip, wrinkling his nose. "Oh. Please, don't share those."

"I won't have to if, and this is a big if, Philip here does a few things for me," David continued, leaning forward so he was closer to the other man.

Philip's jowls shook. "I can only imagine."

"Obviously, you're going to drop this entire thing, and you're going to forget all about it. And then, you're going to request a transfer," David told him.

"To where?" Philip asked.

"I...honestly couldn't care less. So long as you're not on my base, running my operations, and trying to stab me in the back. I'd hoped to find you somewhere nice before all this, but you can scoop shit out of a private's latrine for all it matters to me. I want to find your request for reassignment on my desk within two weeks. I want you out of my sight and out of my hair," David told him.

"You can't bully me out," Phillip shot back.

"I can, and I will. I might be stripped of almost everything if you release what you have, but let's be honest, I've *earned* what I have. And a little dalliance? I might even get away with only losing a little, especially in the face of what they'd have to deal with when it comes to you. I bet you have a sealed history, don't you, Philip? That's probably why you never got higher than you are, and they let me have you because they knew I'd be fair to you. Well, now I'm being fair to everyone."

Philip looked down at his hands, shaking his head. "All this time, you've kept it all this time. I don't believe it."

"Tell you what, Philip, I'll show it to you tomorrow when I'm back at work. I might be a 'noble and honorable man', but that doesn't make me a fool. I always felt a little guilty for keeping hold of that file, but now? I see it was just good instincts."

Philip's hands balled into fists against the counter. David could see everything crumbling down around the man. There would be many questions about why Philip needed such a rapid transfer, and the whispering would begin. Anytime a transfer request was put in, and the superior officer supported it, it was usually a bad sign of internal problems. If Philip really did have the history David suspected, it would undoubtedly come up in the minds of Command when they caught wind. It would hurt Philip, but at least it was better than having everything confirmed.

David wrinkled his nose, tapping the counter. "I'm glad we understand one another. Come to my office tomorrow if you don't believe me. I'll make a believer out of you. Now get the fuck out of my house before I throw you out."

Without a word, Philip stood up, glaring hatefully at him and Christian before stomping out. The slam of the front door echoed through the house as Philip left, and David grinned as he heard the man's heavy steps going down the front porch.

He turned, stopping as he caught sight of the look on Christian's face. "What?"

Christian leaped forward, wrapping his legs around David's waist and hugging his neck. Without a word, Christian kissed him soundly, taking the wind from his lungs with his intensity.

"Oh, hello," David said with a smile.

"Fuck, that was hot," Christian told him.

David chuckled. "I'm glad you approve."

"And then some!"

David wrapped an arm around his waist, holding Christian against him. "Well, let's get your coffee, and then we can talk, just like I promised."

"Shower first, damn it. I'm all sweaty and want to wash the stink of Philip off me."

"Shower first," David agreed.

And he was even more sure of his decision, something he might just thank Philip for later.

CHRISTIAN

Fresh and clean, Christian bounded out of the bathroom and launched himself into the air. With a soft laugh, he landed on the folds of the bed and sprawled out. David's shower had an overhead attachment and three built into the walls. It was large enough to fit both of them very comfortably, and Christian had taken his time with David, making sure they used up all the hot water.

David followed him at a more sedate pace. "I wasn't aware you could fling yourself."

Christian looked up, smirking. "I used to be in track and field back in school. Well, different schools. Geez, there were a lot of school teams I had to try out for now I think about it."

"I never knew you were an athlete," David admitted, toweling off his head.

Christian watched the water drip down David's bare body. "Yeah, I did quite a bit when I could. It helped when I had to hop from school to school, sometimes two or three times a year. Different towns, different schools, different people, different lessons, but I could always count on being able to do track and field, baseball, stuff like that."

David paused, humming appreciatively. "That's right, you're on the baseball team here, aren't you?"

"Why yes, General Winter, I am on one of the teams you created," Christian said with a laugh.

David winced. "Doesn't say good things that I have baseball teams created, with games and space set aside for them, and I've never been to see a single game in years."

Christian chuckled. "Well, everyone's happy you did. It gives us something to do other than get into trouble. You're a pretty busy man, most people get that."

David stopped at the edge of the bed, running a hand over Christian's leg. "If it means a chance to see you in baseball pants, I might just have to make time."

Christian laughed, playfully swatting at David's hand. "You're a pervert, you know that? I thought older guys were supposed to lose some of their libido."

David scowled. "Was that an age joke?"

"Only if it means I'm making fun of myself for being outdone by someone older than me," Christian said.

David bent over him, placing a hand on the bed on each side of Christian. "I stand by blaming you for that."

"Me? What did I do?" Christian protested.

David looked him over, taking his time. "Need I say more?"

Christian reached up, cupping David's face and pulling him down into a sound kiss. "In the year I've known you, I never have imagined you to be a sweet talker."

"I am a man of many skills," David said.

"And boy, am I learning that," Christian replied.

Rather than bringing himself down for the kill, as Christian expected, David flopped down next to him. Christian blinked in surprise but smiled when David curled up on his side, wrapping an arm around Christian's chest.

"You okay?" Christian asked softly.

David closed his eyes, nodding his head. "I will be. That was...unbelievably nerve-wracking. I never thought it was Philip behind Ethan's blackmail attempt."

"Well, not strictly Philip," Christian reminded him.

"True, but if it hadn't been for Philip's attempts to get some dirt on me, Ethan might never have realized the value of what he had."

"And now, neither of them is a problem."

David cracked his eyes open. "And I have you to thank."

Christian gazed into the pale green of David's eyes. They reminded him of old jade. "Maybe Ethan, but you took care of Philip."

David nuzzled into Christian's neck, kissing it. "I just...imagine if it had been anyone else but Philip. All these years I've kept that folder, just in case. I never knew what that case might be, but something told me to keep hold of it and not let it out of my sight."

"I think that means you should be listening to your gut more often," Christian pointed out.

David's eyes flashed open completely, and he smiled. "That's...good advice, and I think I'll do just that."

Christian's chest tightened. "Yeah?"

David tucked an elbow beneath him so he hovered over Christian's face. "Yes. When you originally presented the idea of you and I being more than just a one-night fling, I told you I needed more time to think about it. To weigh the benefits and the risks."

"You did," Christian said, swallowing.

"And I'm realizing that was a clinical way of handling it. It was cold, and I apologize. I should have handled it better."

Christian blinked. "Wait, you're worried that I took offense?"

"It was quite blunt."

Christian laughed. "Yes, and *you* are blunt, you absolute dork."

"Dork?"

Christian continued to laugh, pushing David onto his back so he could lay across him. "I never once took offense to what you said. You're always measuring things against one another, weighing the pros and cons. You think things through and use your brain to make your decisions. That's just who you are, and it's not like I suddenly expected you to be any different because I was asking you to be serious with me. Hell, I would have been shocked if you had an answer right away."

David shook his head, running a hand along Christian's neck. "I suppose you are used to me."

"I am. I know how you operate. And I know what I asked wasn't the easiest thing to think about either. At the end of the day, what we did could put us at risk...and obviously, there was some threat to it. I could and can understand if that threat is too much for you," Christian said softly.

David cupped the back of Christian's head. "I thought much the same thing. It seemed like a monumental risk, and for something we...have no idea will work."

"Your career. Mine," Christian agreed.

"And any future aspirations you might have. That sort of thing could follow you around forever."

"And ruin what you have now."

David nodded. "But I've decided I don't care."

Christian froze. "Wait...really?"

"Of course. I should have known that anyone willing to go to the lengths you did to protect me was worth keeping close. And I should have known it was a sign when I was willing to ignore a strict rule, all for one night with you. And then I should have known when I didn't give you an immediate answer when you asked for something more. There have been a lot of signs pointing me in the direction I've been heading the whole time, but the last piece of the puzzle slipped into place last night."

Christian laughed. "I didn't know the sex was *that* good."

David rolled his eyes. "It wasn't the sex. It was seeing you standing on the balcony by yourself."

Christian wrinkled his nose. "Seriously? I looked like an absolute mess."

"You looked like someone who had been through the wringer, that's true."

"You're...helping my case, not yours here."

David ignored him. "And you looked absolutely amazing to me. I realized I was seeing under all the smart jokes, under the efficient, dedicated workmanship. Past the smiles, the happy-go-lucky attitude and the patience for dealing with everyone all the time. I was seeing the Christian who was worn out, driven half-mad, and fed up with everything. And I realized I wanted nothing more than to draw you close and never let you go. You didn't look like a mess. You looked like a man I could give my heart to."

Christian had teased the general about his inability to give compliments, and now he was fully prepared to take back that comment and never let it loose again. His mouth dried as he stared at David, dumbfounded.

"I...have never had anyone say...anything like that to me before," Christian admitted.

"That's truly a shame. Someone as loyal, hardworking, goodhearted, and joyful deserves to be told it often. You've made my job easier and better, and somewhere along the line, you started doing the same for my life. So what I'm asking, Christian, is if you'll do the same for my heart," David said, voice petering off into a whisper.

It wouldn't be easy, not by a long shot. Their relationship would have to be strictly controlled, locked away from the rest of the world. At work, they could never once slip up, carefully watching what they said and did around one another, watchful for a wrong look or inappropriate comment. They would never be allowed to eat out together, go to the beach, or simply walk the streets hand in hand.

As long as they were in their positions, their entire relationship would have to be a secret. Yet, as much as Christian believed in living his life out in the open, he couldn't ignore how much he wanted the man in front of him. David was a rock, something Christian could hold fast to and stay grounded. The man was true to his word, more kindhearted than he gave himself credit for, and more dedicated to his duty than anyone Christian had ever seen.

He was a skillful lover and a kind man. And he was asking Christian to be with him. Secret relationship or not, he knew what his heart wanted.

Christian bent forward, kissing him softly. "Yes, I will."

EPILOGUE

One Year Later

David hummed as he marched down the path to his home. He'd stayed later in the office than he would have liked, but he had to make a few last-minute adjustments. His assistant was not the most adept and struggled under the job's demands. As such, David was forced to take on a great deal, which increased his already substantial workload.

However, it wasn't all bad, as his work had been gradually reduced over the past few months. His gut feeling for Oscar Reyes had turned out to be on the money. The man had proven very good at the job once he'd gotten a handle on the full scope of his duties. David quickly found many responsibilities he'd taken over for Operations slipping back where they belonged and straight into Reyes' capable hands.

David stopped at the gate, gazing up at his home with a frown. It wasn't the first time in the past couple of months that he'd spent longer at work than usual. In truth, he could have dealt with everything the next day but chose to stay in the office. His house felt so lonely without Christian around to spend a few nights a week with him.

For almost a decade, David had loved the peace and quiet of his house. Then he'd begun dating Christian, and his home was filled with glorious noise three to four times a week. Christian loved music when he did just about anything and loved singing along. He was also fond of dancing to the music, whether or not he was clothed. Then there were constant conversations, with Christian always ready to fill the silence and talk to David about anything and everything, approaching every subject happily and excitedly. David's peace had been shattered and replaced with something infinitely more valuable.

Life.

But now, Christian was gone. Studying law in Boston. It had been a hard decision for him, but inevitably, he'd decided a military career was not for him. The last week of Christian's time at Fort Dale had been beautiful, filled with desperate lovemaking and bittersweet talks long into the night. Yet, he'd had to leave, flying out to move in with his sisters, who were overjoyed to have their brother around.

David sighed, swinging the gate open and walking up the front path. They still talked, of course, and video-called when they could. Messages were shot back and forth all day, some clean and some not. David had no problem sharing compromising pictures of himself with Christian, something the other man found both arousing and amusing, considering David's history.

Unlocking the front door, he stepped inside, dropped his bag, and flipped on the light.

"Honey, I'm home," he called into the empty space.

A head popped up from the darkness of the living room. "Hi, honey."

David stumbled back, gripping the doorway. "Jesus Christ!"

Christian's laughter echoed through the house. "Someone's jumpy. Maybe you should cut down on the caffeine."

David brought a hand to his furiously pounding heart. "Good Lord, Christian, you scared the sense out of me."

"I can tell," Christian said, flopping over the back of the couch with a devilish grin.

"You are aware I'm nearing fifty, right? You could give me a heart attack," David accused as he stepped closer.

Christian looked up at him, frowning. "That's not funny. And considering your ticker is still as good as ever, highly unlikely."

"How did...which one was it?"

"Troy."

David sighed. "I will be having a little talk with him."

"Like hell you are. I have the goods on him."

David raised a brow. "The goods?"

"Yep."

"Oh goody, now you're having clandestine talks with my medics."

Christian hopped over the back of the couch and immediately darted for David. Knowing what was coming, David held his arms out, grunting as Christian's body collided with his. Christian slid his arms around David's neck and held tight, grinning.

"I missed you," Christian whispered.

David's frown melted away. "I missed you."

It had only been a few months, but it felt like an eternity since he'd held Christian in his arms. He was warm in every way the word could be used, and his weight against David felt like a drowning man's first breath. David pulled him closer, savoring their first sweet kiss in three months.

"So much," David added against his lips.

"Good," Christian said, running a thumb against the base of David's neck.

"How did you get here?" David asked, still holding tight to him.

"It's Spring Break. I've got two whole weeks all to myself. My sisters wanted to do something, but all I had to say was I was gonna come here, and they shut right up. Lily says hi and that she can't wait to meet you. And I'm sorry, but she'll probably call you Daddy Winter," Christian added with a grimace.

David blinked. "Pardon?"

"Don't ask. And when she does, don't react. Otherwise, it'll just encourage her."

"I'm not sure if I should be offended or not."

"Don't be. You'll like Mary more. Well, once she pulls off the big sister act, she swears she won't do it, but she will anyway."

David raised a brow. "I'm glad you didn't choose sales as your vocation. You're not good at that."

"I sold you on me, though, didn't I?" Christian asked with a wicked grin.

"That you did."

"And now you get me for a whole two weeks, all to yourself."

David hummed. "You know, I could probably get away with taking the next two weeks off."

"Seriously? Oscar's been that good?"

"Oh, yes. And I'm overdue for a vacation."

Christian's blue eyes lit up with excitement. "Two weeks of just us, here and being us?"

David grinned. "Christian. You're not stationed here anymore. You're not my subordinate."

"Out of bed," Christian said with a grin.

David ignored him, even as his gut tightened at the thought. "We don't have to be a secret anymore."

"Oh. Shit, you're right," Christian said with widening eyes.

David nodded. "So, yes, two weeks of us being here, being us. But two weeks of me taking you out to eat at my favorite places you can't get takeout from. Two weeks of trips to the beach, seeing shows, or just walking around and enjoying the weather."

Christian stared up at him in wonder. "I...had got so used to it. I never realized we were free."

David kissed him. "I can finally show off the man I love."

"And so can I," Christian murmured against his lips.

But it was late, and he had Christian in his arms with every intention of keeping him there for hours. They could face the next day with new possibilities, no longer forced to keep themselves secret. David was going to take advantage of every moment and love every minute of living their life, showing their love, out in front of the world without a care.

ABOUT THE AUTHOR

Romeo Alexander lives in Michigan, USA, with his dog and two cats. As a certified night owl, coffee and a wicked sense of humor keep him going most days, as does playing with flavors in the kitchen.

As a gay man, he believes in writing about what you know whenever possible; his stories come from the heart and with a dose of humor thrown in. His characters grapple with relationships, emotions, and real-world issues, good and bad, using their hearts as a guiding compass to get their all-important happy ever after.

Printed in Great Britain
by Amazon